Disturbed:

An Unbalanced Love
Part Two

A Novel By

Myiesha

WITHDRAWN FROM
RAPIDES PARISH LIBRARY

RAPIDES PARISH LIBRARY
Alexandria, Louisiana

Text ROYALTY to 42828 to join our mailing list!

To submit a manuscript for our review, email us at submissions@royaltypublishinghouse.com

Text RPHCHRISTIAN to 22828

for our CHRISTIAN ROMANCE novels!

Text RPHROMANCE to 22828
for our INTERRACIAL ROMANCE novels!

LEGAL NOTES

© 2016

Published by Royalty Publishing House

http://www.royaltypublishinghouse.com

ALL RIGHTS RESERVED.

This is a work of fiction. Names, characters, businesses, places, events and incidents are either the products of the author's imagination or used in a fictitious manner. Any resemblance to actual persons, living or dead, or actual events is purely coincidental. Unauthorized

LODI

"How was that?" I asked Venus, who was now lying on top of me out of breath.

"That was amazing, baby," she said.

"It definitely was," I agreed. We've been trying out new positions since we discovered that she turned whenever I was on top of her. We've discovered some pretty creative positions, so much so that I was thinking about marketing them shits. It's been a month since the miscarriage and we were back at it again. She had become a fucking sex machine. She felt so good I consistently had to stop myself from putting a baby up in her gut again. But I also wanted to respect her wishes and wait until she was ready.

"Round four," I asked her.

"No, I need a quick break," she said, getting up off the bed. I grabbed her back down and laid on top of her.

"How long have we been living together, Venus?" I asked her.

"I don't know... about three, maybe four months," she answered.

"Those four months feels like forever."

"That's because we got at least four years of friendship."

"Yeah, I guess you can say that," I said.

"I know I said it in letters, but I don't think I've told you verbally that I love you, Venus. Every time I wrote it in a letter I meant it, and every time I say it, I will mean it."

She looked up at me.

"I love you too, Lodi. I have always loved you ever since we were in detention," she responded.

"I know it may be too early to be speaking of this now, but I'm going to make you my wife someday. Maybe not today, maybe not tomorrow, but I will."

"Not before I make you my husband," she said, kissing me on the mouth.

"Oh yeah, you plan on dropping to your knee and proposing to me?" I asked her.

"If I have to I will. I don't see no trouble in doing that."

"You crazy, girl, you know that?" I asked her.

"Yes I do, I'm the one who told you I was crazy," she said.

"I'm crazy in love with you, Ladonis Omari Dawson."

"I really have to stop you from hanging with my mother. She done told you my middle name and I don't know yours."

"That's because you never asked," she said, pushing me off her.

"Okay, I'm asking now, what's your middle name?"

"None of your business," she said walking away.

"Oh no, no, no, get over here and tell me your middle name," I said, getting up off the bed and grabbing her. I started tickling her because I knew she would have wanted me to stop and I wasn't until she told me her middle name.

"Okay, okay, okay," she said, out of breath from laughing.

"It's Alana," she relented.

"Venus Alana Morgan, I like that. May I ask you why you are

ashamed of it?"

"Because my mother's name is Jessica Alana Morgan. I would prefer not to be named after the woman who made my life hell."

"Well, I think it's a nice name no matter whose name it is. It's beautiful and it fits your beautiful soul," I said, kissing her on the nose.

"Let's go get some food, I'm starving," she said, heading over to the closet to look for clothes.

"Are you really starving or you just want something in your mouth, cuz we just ate like two hours ago? I think you have Freud's Theory of Oral Fixation," I said, dropping some knowledge.

"Ok, college grad, what's oral fixation?" she asked.

"Oral fixation is a condition when a person always has to have something in their mouth, whether it's eating or chewing something, like Loc and his pen caps," I said. She sat there thinking for a bit.

"Hmmm, maybe you're right, but then again, maybe I could just be hungry, you ever thought about that? Now, can we please go get something to eat," she said, whining like a little baby.

"Fine, let me put some clothes on," I said, walking over to the closet with her.

****

We were dressed and headed downstairs. I said "what up" to Joe the doorman before we exited the building.

"So what is it that you want to eat?" I asked Venus.

7

"Whatever. It doesn't really matter, I'm just hungry."

"It doesn't matter, huh? So how about some warm shit balls and rice?"

"Why do you have to be so nasty all the time?"

"What I tell you about saying whatever? Make up your mind. What do you have a taste for?"

"How about Mexican?" she suggested.

"That's cool with me. There's an authentic Mexican restaurant on Route 46 that we can go to. I heard they got some bomb fajitas," I said.

"Cool, I can go for chicken fajita and a Pina Colada," she said.

"Since when you became a fan of alcohol?" I asked her because I tried getting her to drink before and she never did.

"Since I got with you."

"I don't even drink that much," I said.

"Yeah, well you stressed me out that much that I now need to drink."

"Whatever," I said, lightly pushing her then grabbing her back and pulling her into my arms as we crossed the street. I was giving her a wet willy, when I heard car tires screeching towards us. I looked up and there was a car heading straight towards us.

"Shit," I said pushing her out the street. By the time I thought about getting myself out of danger, the front end of the car came straight at me, hitting me, sending me flying at least eight feet into the air.

VENUS

I got myself up off the ground, looking around for Lodi.

"Someone call 9-1-1," I heard a woman yell. I allowed my eyes to follow where she was running towards.

I gathered myself and ran down the street to see what was going on. It was Lodi. He was lying in the street not moving. I got closer and he was bleeding. Looking at him, my knees became weak.

"Lodi, baby, wake up, please," I cried while shaking him. But he wasn't waking up. "Lodi," I cried again. Lodi was the only person I had in this world, now he was on the verge of leaving me. This couldn't be happening. I cried and cried and continued to cry, until I felt myself about to throw up. I turned around and let it all out.

"Ma'am, are you ok?" the woman asked me. I wiped my mouth and gathered myself. I reached in his pocket for his phone so that I could call his parents and Loc. When I opened up the phone, his messages immediately opened up. It wasn't my intention on reading the message, but something caught my eyes. It was a message from Kim saying that she was pregnant. My head started spinning, my vision became faint, and my world became black.

MARS

I look down at Lodi's body and he wasn't looking too good. He had blood coming from his nose, his mouth, and his ears. One of his legs was twisted behind his body in a way that a human body should never twist. There was blood also coming from behind his head. I sat there admiring the scene. I felt a small smile creep up on my face.

"Hey, baby love," I heard from behind me. Recognizing the voice, I became excited. I turned around and there he stood. I stood up and walked in his direction.

"You're responsible for this?" I asked him with a smile.

"I'm responsible for a lot of things. Sorry about your boyfriend, Miss Venus," he said, smiling back at me.

"He's not my boyfriend and my name's not Venus. It's Mars, baby, you know that."

"So it's you?" he asked.

"You damn right, baby," I said walking up to him.

"You weren't lying when you said you were disturbed."

"Nope, I wasn't. You still looking for a shoota, boo?"

"I think I might have already found her. How about we go get lost together, baby love?"

"Let's ride."

MARS

"Aye little girl, don't be changing my shit," Trub said, slapping my hand off the radio. I slapped his hand back and continued flipping through the stations. Trub and I had been together for the last few weeks with no sign of Venus's punk ass. This was starting to feel like a permanent thing. It could have been the fact that we'd been getting into all kinds of shit and loving every minute of it. It was like He Say, She Say. He says blast and I'm laying niggas out. I say kill 'em and he's planting a bullet in the middle of their dome for me. With him I felt unstoppable. We were double fucking trouble. Fuck Bonnie and Clyde. If we ever came across them, we would lay their assess out too. Not a duo around could fuck with me and my nigga.

"For one, Najavar, I don't want to listen to that bullshit, and two," I was saying before he interrupted me.

"What you mean, bullshit? Man, Jada and DMX, this some certifiable gangsta shit, little girl."

When it rains, niggaz get wet, so stay dry
Don't cross me, I can peek the snake eye
Just lost you, left your shadow in the dark
Fucked around it forced me to hit the shadow with a spark
Blew your shit apart, now it's two halves of one nigga
"Look at him," I said after a few laughs, "Dumb nigga
Stupid is as stupid does cocksucker
And look what being stupid does, get you shot sucker.

I let you get too close and you bit me

I suppose it went on for too long you tried to hit me

Thought you was wit me

Well you might as well forget me, cuz from this point on

It's war, it won't stop until one of us is gone

I'm still mad at myself for lettin that shit go down

Somebody shoulda told me I was fuckin wit a clown

And I think they found and let... you... nigga... drown

...you know how shit get around. "

He was going hard, rapping the lyrics like the shit was personal. For some reason, I couldn't stop myself from staring at those sexy, thick, pink lips of his, and that brown skin complexion and those neat dreads that flowed down his back. He always seemed to smell like baby powder or baby's breath or something innocent when ironically, nothing about him was innocent.

"Why ya weird ass staring at me like that?" he asked, breaking me from my trance.

"Anyway, it's trash, and two, I ain't a little girl, I'm a grown ass woman. Get it right," I said, snapping my fingers at him.

"What makes you think you're grown; you don't even know who you are. Remember, you're not even a real person."

"Word, that's how you feeling right now? So would a not so real little girl do this?" I said, taking off my seat belt and placing my knees in the seat. I turned towards him and reached over and started fumbling with his pants. I unbuckled his belt, zipping down his pants and unleashing my dear friend, who I've become close within the last few weeks. I ducked under his right arm that was on the steering wheel, and placed him inside my mouth like I did with Lodi on the many nights I switched during him and Venus's sex sessions. Trub wasn't as big as Lodi, but he wasn't small either. I would say he was perfectly right to have fun with. I bobbed my head up and down with his hard member sliding in and out of my mouth. I had to say I was really becoming an expert at this activity.

"Oh shit, girl," he said, followed by a moan. Hearing that he was enjoying it made me start sucking him harder and faster. I felt the car swerve and I popped my head up.

"Girl, you about to make me crash this car," he said, pushing my head back down.

"You want me to stop?"

"Hell no, just keep doing what you doing, baby luv. Whoaa, Jesus take the motherfucking wheel," he uttered as I continued to do what I was doing. I continued until I felt his private start to pulsate and I felt his salty liquid shoot down my throat.

When he was done, I came back up for air. I hadn't even realized he had pulled over. I wiped around my mouth and pulled down the mirror.

"How was that for a little girl, nigga?"

"That shit was the bomb, baby luv. Where the hell did you learn to give head like that from, girl?" Trub asked.

"I watched someone do it when I was in detention and I kind of figured out the purpose of it." I avoided telling him the truth that I had done it a few times on Lodi; he probably would have put the car back in drive and pushed me out of the moving car. I didn't know why they had so much animosity towards one another.

Tap, tap. I turned towards the window and there was someone standing there in a hot pink dress, but they were so tall that I couldn't see their face. I had to bend down and look up into the incredibly tall woman's face. Well, I think it was woman. I proceeded to roll down the window.

"Can I help you?" I asked it.

"Excuse me, but if anyone is going to be sucking dick on this block, it'll be me, bitch. This is my turf, hoe," the person bickered. I looked at it in the face and then turned and looked at Trub who was laughing his ass off.

"Did this he-man really just insinuate that I was tricking?"

"Yes the hell I did, fish. Why the hell else would you be outside sucking a nigga off?"

"Hold the hell up," I said reaching over in Trub's waistband, pulling out his gun and opening the door and getting out.

"Oh what, you wanna fight, bitch? Let's go then, turf war motherfucker," the tall he woman provoked, backing up from the car. She snatched off her wig and walked it over to the gate and hung it up, along with her purse. She dropped her fake fur to the ground and proceeded to walk up to me with her fists up like the nigga she was. I waited until he-she got closer and I pulled the gun out from behind my back and aimed it straight in the middle of her forehead.

"Ahhhh," she screamed, clutching on to her pearls.

"You wanna repeat what you just said, sir-ma'am."

"I was just joking, sis, calm down. You can't take a joke sister, girl? You know what, let me just get my shit and be on my way. I had no business getting up into y'alls business anyway. I really need to learn to start minding my damn business, and today is the day I turn over a new leaf," the big woman said, placing her wig back on her head, picking up the fake fur coat and walking away as fast as her little plastic heels would allow her. I put the gun away and climbed back into the car.

"Damn, you were about to get yo' ass beat by a tranny," Trub joked.

"Yea, whatever. That tranny was about to catch a bullet in her ass fucking with me. She might have liked it."

"You really are a fucking nut. Look at yo' eyes, them shits black. I've never seen anyone with black eyes. You the only one, you and Satan. You are the product of Satan," Trub said, placing a blunt to his lips and lighting it.

"You could be right. Give me some of that and let's go before I have to shoot somebody out this bitch."

****

Minutes later, we were pulling up to Dr. Burke's office. He had been blowing Venus's cell phone up stating she'd missed some of her appointments.

"Aight, ma, give me that," Trub demanded, taking the blunt from out of my mouth.

"What you do that for?" I asked him, sitting up from my

slouching position.

"Because you need to get focused and get on your Venus shit, aight? This man is trained to read through people. Any fuck ups, Venus ass is going right back to the nut house and guess what? Yo' ass is going right along with her. How we gon' be the Bonnie and Clyde of New Jersey with you locked in a straitjacket?" Trub asked.

"Alright, alright," I said, pulling down the mirror and checking myself out.

I picked up the container that held the contacts and opened it.

"Ok, how do I do this?" I asked, looking down at the creepy green color contacts floating in the solution. Trub took the case out of my hands and proceeded to put them in for me.

Dr. Burke has been treating Venus and I for years now. I had a few encounters with him, which ended in me being taken out of his office in restraints. Dr. Burke knew all there was to know about Venus, from the way that she walked to how she sat.

I was trying to trick Dr. Burke into believing that I was Venus, so I had to change a few things for the session.

"You know, for a badass stickup kid, you're pretty gentle," I coaxed. He didn't respond at first, he just continued what he was doing and then sat back in his seat.

"Don't offend me, I'm a motherfucking G, aight?"

"Yea, whatever. How I look?" I asked him.

"Like yourself with green contacts in," Trub remarked. I sucked my teeth.

"Whatever. Let me go in here and play miserable," I said, getting out the car, shutting the door and walking towards the building.

"Yo," Trub called from the car. I turned around.

"Straighten that back, shawty. Venus doesn't slouch."

"And you know this how?" I quizzed.

"I was following them for weeks. Now up straight and take that switch out ya hips, chicken head." I gave him the finger, rolled my eyes and turned back around. I stood up straight and started stiffly walking back to the door. When I got inside, I started looking around for Dr. Burke's office. I spotted the nameplate on the door and started towards it.

"Venus!" I heard someone happily call. I turned around and the peppy receptionist jumped out of her seat a little too excited.

Who the fuck is this bitch? I thought to myself, as the woman came over and gave me a hug. I put on my biggest, fakest smile, and embraced the woman back. That's what Venus would have done.

"How you doing today, V?"

"I'm cool. Is Dr. Burke ready for me? I'm kinda in a rush," I said.

"Sure thing, let me just let him know you're here," she giggled, as she reached over to her phone and called Dr. Burke's office. Before she could even turn back around, I walked off towards the office and bust right through the door . He looked up from his desk with a confused look on his face. *Shit, that wasn't Venus like,*

I thought.

"Uh, hello Venus, yes, come in why don't you," he said, looking at me suspiciously.

"Hello, Dr. Burke," I said shyly.

"How's everything?"

"Everything is good, I'm just in a rush. I have a friend waiting for me," I said, making up an excuse for my rude actions.

"Ok, well let's get started," he said pointing to the chair. I walked over and plopped down in the chair and leaned back with my arm over the back of the chair on some nigga shit.

"Ooo k," he said, analyzing my posture. When I realized what he was looking at, I sat up straight with both of my hands on my lap, now in full Venus mode.

"I've been good, Dr. Burke. I've been taking my medication faithfully. I'm sorry I haven't been here for my sessions; transportation has played a major role in my absence. Everything is great. I haven't had any bad thoughts, no Mars since I left the facility. I'm perfectly ok," I said, trying to speed up this tedious process.

"Since you left? The last time you were here you told me about an incident that you had at a nightclub. You also expressed to me that your medication may not be working," Dr. Burke said.

"Oh yea, I meant since that time. That was only one time and it wasn't for that long." Dr. Burke sat there quietly, looking at me while playing with the pen that was in his hand.

"Good. Are you still residing with your friend, Ladonis

Dawson, at 74 JFK Boulevard, in Jersey City, New Jersey?" he questioned.

"Yes, that's correct," I said, playing with my nails. I felt him look up at me then back down at the file in front of him. He wrote something down and then shut the file.

"You sure everything is ok, Venus?"

"Yes, I'm sure," I answered.

"Good. So I guess I'll see you next week then?"

"Great! Next week it is," I said, jumping up and running out the office. I walked back into the receptionist area.

"Done already, Venus?" the happy front desk lady asked.

"Yep, bye," I said, throwing up a hand and running out the front door.

Trub was still waiting in front of the building. I ran to the car and jumped in through the window, placing a kiss on his lips.

"You're done that quick?" he asked.

"Yep, let's be out," I answered, getting completely into the car.

"How did it go?" he asked, looking at me oddly.

"Good, now let's go," I said, pulling the mirror down, and removing the contacts. I felt him still staring at me.

"Uh, why isn't the car moving?" I asked. He shook his head and started the car. I took the last contact out, put it inside the case, then reached around and put my seat belt on. I looked up at the building and made eye contact with Dr. Burke, who was looking out his office window. *He's gonna become a problem*, I thought, as Trub pulled away from the curb.

A half an hour later, Trub and I were pulling in the projects. We hopped out the car and were walking up to the building, when LD, one of Trub's lookouts, came running up to him.

"What's up, Trub? What's up, beautiful lady?" he said to me, winking his eye and smiling at me. He was too cute. This kid had to be about 13 and he was fearless as hell. If I had a son, he had to be just like him. This kid was too fearless though; he was standing here flirting with me without a care in the world, while my presence had grown men half his age scared to even look me in the eyes.

"Aye, aye, aye, enough of that, little nigga, before I hang you from the fence. What's been going on? Why it's so empty out here?" Trub asked.

"Man, those fucking pigs," LD started saying, until Trub cut him off.

"What the fuck I tell yo' little ass about cursing? Don't make me whoop yo' ass. I told you don't do what I do, do better, lil' nigga. Someone gotta make it out the 'jects and that's gonna be you. You can't be my lawyer talking like that. Now, start over with better word choices," Trub preached. I was a little confused by Trub's speech. As he was preaching better word choices to LD, every word out of his mouth was a curse word.

"The police pulled up talking about stop and frisk and started shaking niggas down. Good thing no one was packing really. They just got Brink for a few bags of weed. Dre, Mack and Von were able to get inside the building so they were good, but P, man,

Peabo spazzed the hell out. You know he's like the guardian of the galaxy when you're not around. He saw them shaking the block and got pissed. He choked out one of the cops, so they booked him. Ma dukes went down there to get him though."

"Why no one called me about this shit?" Trub asked.

"Nigga, we tried to, ya damn phone was going to voicemail," LD stated, causing Trub to dig inside his pocket and pull out his phone that was indeed dead.

"Shit, man. LD, let me see your phone?" Trub asked. LD pulled his phone out and gave it to Trub, who walked away leaving LD and myself standing there.

I felt LD looking at me, so I looked over at him. He was standing there smiling and squinting his eyes seductively. I started laughing at the little nugget head little boy.

"What you looking at?" I asked him.

"You, pretty thang," he flirted.

"So why they call you LD?" I questioned.

"It stands for Little Dude with a long di—" he began saying, but choked on his words from a smack to the back of his head by Trub.

"Watch ya mouth, little nigga. Here," Trub handed him back his phone.

"Get back to work and stop at my car and get that Malcolm X book I picked up for you."

Trub grabbed my hand as we started walking to the building. I couldn't help but stare at him. He was starting to turn out nothing

23

like I thought. On the outside, he had this tough exterior but on the inside, he actually had a soft spot.

"The fuck you looking at?" he asked, catching me staring at him.

"You, nigga. With ya mushy ass," I responded, pushing him.

"Yea, aight, I ain't that mushy. Only for those I care about."

"Uh huh," I said, rolling my eyes as we continued walking through the yard and up to the building.

As we entered the building, I felt someone grab me. I looked down at my arm and there was a boney, ashy hand holding on to it. I looked up to see who wanted to lose their hand for putting it on me and I stood there stunned. I thought I was seeing a ghost.

"Venus, baby girl," she said reaching up with her boney ass arms and hugging me. I didn't embrace the hug, I just stood there stiffly until she let me go.

When she was done, she looked up at me and we made eye contact.

"You still can't tell the difference between the two of us," I said with a devilish smirk on my face. She backed up from me and her smile disappeared as she screwed her face up at me.

"Mars, you evil, demented bitch. Why can't you just leave my daughter be? You're the one stopping her from living a normal life," Jessica raged. I couldn't help but laugh at her.

"No, you're the reason why she can't have a normal life. You created me because you were a shitty ass mother. You should have just aborted her when you found out you were pregnant. She would

24

have had a better life being birthed by a dog," I retorted.

I guess those words hit a soft spot because she came charging at me. I swung my purse and hit her upside her head, which sent her frail, under 100-pound body, stumbling into the wall and then on to the floor.

"Yo' ass ain't get enough of putting your hands on me? Last time you almost lost a hand, right? All I had to do was apply a little bit more pressure and I would have had that ass walking around here like Candyman. Did you ever find out what happened to the man you let rape Venus?" I asked, squatting down to her level and getting closer to her, now whispering to prevent the crowd that had formed around us, from hearing me.

"I murdered his ass. Cut his dick off and set the house on fire. Keep on playing with me, you'll be next, crackhead."

"Bitch," she said raising her arm and slapping the shit out of me. I fell flat on my ass, stunned that this crackhead had so much power in her boney ass arm. I raised my foot and kicked her straight in her forehead, sending her head smacking against the wall. I stood up and started stomping and kicking her all over her body.

"Aight, baby luv, it's cool," Trub said, coming behind me and grabbing me by the waist. I brushed my hair from in front of my face and started walking away from her. I looked around at the crowd of people that was standing around. There was one girl whose face stood out. We made eye contact and it was something familiar about those eyes that I couldn't quite put my finger on, and for some reason, I couldn't tear my eyes from hers. We stared each other down until Trub pulled me on to the elevator and the doors shut.

TRUB

I sat in the window of Ma Dukes apartment, staring out into the parking lot waiting on her and Peabo to pull up. Ma Dukes was like the hood mother. She took in everyone and treated us all like we were her very own. She took me in when I was nine years old. I had parents, but they were both arrested and accused of being kingpins back when I was seven. My mother was serving 15 years, and my father was serving 20 years. When they were arrested, I was left to provide for myself. I was a smart little nigga back then. I knew if they had found me, they would have placed me in foster care with some lame ass family, and I wasn't beat for that shit at all, so I bounced.

After they arrested my parents, I was able to sneak back into the house and grab my blue crayon bank which was where I would save my weekly allowance that I received from my father. I had saved up $376, which I used to get me through the first year on the streets. After I spent all of my allowance, I had to find other ways of survival. I started robbing people and stealing from supermarkets to eat. That's how I ran into Ma Dukes.

I was in Certified Supermarket, strolling the cereal and oodles and noodles aisle. I had already managed to get a quart of milk in my book bag and a box of fruit snacks before someone came on the aisle. I wanted a box of Trix, but there was this one lady that wouldn't leave the aisle for shit. So I moved down to the next aisle where the noodles were. I took two packs of beef noodles and stuffed them in my pants without getting seen. I went back over to the cereal aisle and the lady that had been standing there forever was leaving out the same way I was coming. She looked me dead in my face and we made eye contact, until she turned the corner to the next aisle. I walked up to the Trix and grabbed the smallest box. I looked down both ends of the aisle before stuffing it inside my book bag. I started walking out the aisle when the lady came back, stopping me in my tracks. She blocked the aisle with her cart so I turned to go out the other way. When I turned, she swiftly grabbed the hook of my book bag and snatched it off my back, and unzipped it. I worked too hard and was damn near close to victory, so I reached for my bag and tried to grab it back. She dug in and took out the cereal.

"That's mine," I said, struggling with the book bag.

"What, Trix are not just for kids?" she said, throwing the box in her cart. She reached in for the rest of the stolen items and I pulled even harder, as she let go and sent me flying to the ground. She put the other items in her cart and walked over to me.

"Give me the stuff you have in your pants," she said with her hands out.

"No," I shouted, refusing to give it up.

"Either you give it to me or I'm going to go tell store security, and you're going to go to jail like your parents."

"How do you know my parents?" I asked.

"Don't worry about all that, now give them here and let's go pay for it," she demanded with her hands still held out. I pulled the

two packs of noodles out my pants and handed them to her. She started walking back to her cart and threw them in.

"Let's go," she said and I followed her. She paid for all my stuff and handed me my bag. The least I could do was help her put her bags in her car.

"Where have you been staying?" she asked. I looked at her and didn't answer her question. I didn't need her knowing I didn't have anywhere to stay.

"I'm not going to hand you in to DYFS or anything. I just need to know for the next time I speak with ya father. He's been worried about you."

"How do you know my parents? I've never seen you before."

"Hun, ya momma, father and I used to work together. I should have been right next to them in prison but lucky for me, I didn't get caught. I have been keeping their commissary full though.

I recognized you the first time you peeked ya little bean head down the aisle. I knew I recognized that face, but I couldn't be too sure until the second time. I knew right off the back that it was you. You look just like ya momma."

"What's my name then?" I questioned her. She stood there looking at me with her hand on her hips and a lit cigarette in her other hand. She took a pull then tossed it on the ground and stepped on it.

"Najavar Ishmel Young, birthday January 21, 1992, born at 8:02 in the morning at Barnet Hospital. Mother name Nancy Flores and father name is Ishmel Young; Big Daddy Ish is what the

ladies called him." I stood there looking at her. She really did know me and my parents. I turned and continued putting the bags away.

"I haven't really been staying in one place. Some days I'm here, some days I'm there. My favorite place, though, is the abandoned building on Oak and Summer Street."

"Where were you staying before the streets?" she questioned.

"Nowhere. I've always been in the streets. I have my ways to survive though. My dad taught me well."

"So you been living on the streets for the last two years. I cannot believe this shit," she said, slamming the trunk of her car.

"It's cool. I'm good Miss. Next time you talk to my father let him know I'm doing good."

"Get yo' butt in this car. What kind of friend would I be to let you continue to stay on the streets? And don't call me Miss, call me Ma Dukes," she said.

Since then, she's been nothing less than a mother to me. She raised me to be the person I am today. A stone cold ruthless motherfucker. I watch Ma Dukes cut off niggas' fingers, eyelids, set bitches' hair on fire, and I've enjoyed every moment of it.

I was brought out of my daydream by the touch of Mars's soft hand.

"You alright, baby?" she asked.

"Yea, I was just thinking. You alright, killa?" I asked her.

"I'm cool," she answered dryly.

"I don't know, you put a whooping on that fiend downstairs.

That was ya moms?"

"I don't have a mom, I'm not a real person, remember? That was Venus's mom."

"Yeah, however that goes. It seems like there's a lot of hatred between you two."

"Yep. She traded Venus to a man for drugs when Venus was 10. She sat there and watched as this man raped her own daughter. That piece of shit woman down there is a disgrace to the human race. Back then, I was more like Venus's protector, her guardian from all things bad, so whenever she found herself in situations she couldn't handle, I was there to handle them. I protected her from bullies and rapist and I protected her from her junkie mother. I started killing when I, well, when we were nine years old. My first victim was a cat," she confessed.

"A cat? What the fuck was wrong with ya crazy ass? I guess it's true when they say cruelty to animals is the first sign of a psychopath," I stated.

"Yeah, I guess so. I hung it from the roof by a telephone wire that I used to jump rope with. It was days, maybe even weeks before anyone recognized it. I hung it up from the building across from mine, facing my bedroom window. My next body was the wife of the guy that raped Venus. I have a lot of bodies under my belt because of Venus's punk ass," she spoke. I just looked at her and shook my head. Mars was stone cold, and I loved it.

"You crazy, girl," I responded.

"You still around, so I can't be that bad," she said flirtatiously as she walked up to me.

"That's because I'm attracted to crazy, little girl," I said, pulling her by her waist closer to me. She took my hat off and started fingering my scalp through my dreads.

"I got ya crazy, nigga," she purred, putting her hands inside my pants and grabbing on to my dick through my boxers.

"Mmm, what you gonna do with all this dick, huh, baby luv?"

"Why don't you just sit right here and let me show you," she said, walking me into the kitchen and sitting me down in one of the kitchen chairs. She undid my belt and unbuttoned my pants. She pulled out my now hard dick, as she dropped down to her knees. She took my whole dick into her mouth and went to work. Ten minutes into it, I came down her throat twice and I was still rock hard. She stood up and hiked her tight, form fitting dress up, and slid down her laced midnight blue panties. She threw one leg over mine so she was now standing over me. She slowly lowered herself down on to me and started bouncing up and down on me. She switched motions and was now rocking her hips back and forth with me fully inside of her. My breath was getting caught in my throat from the feeling of her walls gripping my shit so tight.

"Breathe, baby," she seductively whispered in my ear, never missing a beat.

"I can't. You suffocating the hell out my dick right now with all this good stuff," I said, picking her up and walking her to the table. I laid her down on the table and started pounding inside of her, delivering stroke after stroke, going deeper and deeper until I couldn't take it anymore. I bust inside of her without a care in the world. I collapsed on top of her, sweaty and out of breath.

"Now what if you had broken somebody's table?"

"I would have just brought her a new one."

"Her? Whose house is this?" she asked.

"All this time we been here and now you wanna know whose house it is?" I asked her. She didn't say anything, just gave me that evil Mars glare.

"It's Ma Dukes' house."

"Your mother?" she asked.

"Something like that," I responded, just as we heard talking coming from the outside of the door and then keys fumbling at the lock.

"Oh shit," I said, pulling out of her quickly and pulling my pants up. I helped her off the table and she pulled down her skirt.

"Where did my panties go?" she asked, looking around the floor for them. I started helping her just as the door came open, and we both darted over to the couch and sat down. Ma Dukes and Peabo walked in the house and into the living room.

"Hey," Ma Dukes said, walking over to the coffee table and putting her purse and keys down.

"Hey, Ma," I responded back to her and she just looked at me. I got up and leaned over and kissed her on the cheek.

"That's more like it. Why you so sweaty and who's this cutie sitting over there looking guilty about something?" she asked. I looked over at Mars and laughed.

"Ma Dukes, this is my friend, Mars. Mars, this is Ma Dukes," I said introducing the two of them.

"Nice to meet you," Mars said, getting up and shaking her hand.

"You're the tiny one who put the beat down on Jessica Do It All?"

"Jessica Do It All?" Mars asked.

"Yep. Because she'll do it all for a hit," Ma said followed by a laugh. I just shook my head at her and her bluntness, but Mars found it hysterical.

"All including selling her daughter for a hit," Mars laughed. Ma Dukes stopped laughing and looked at Mars.

"Wait, Jessica did have a daughter named after a planet. That was you?"

"No, that was Venus, I'm Mars," she said. Ma Dukes looked at her strangely and then looked over at me.

"Really? I don't remember her having another child and my nosey ass knows everyone's business around here."

"Oh, no see, I'm—" Mars started explaining but I cut her off.

"So nigga, what the fuck happened which yo' ass? What I tell you about stepping to them fucking pigs. You ain't learn? Those niggas shoot first, ask questions later, and then plant evidence to justify their actions. You got to be smart, nigga," I preached to Peabo.

"Yea, I know, man. That shit had me hot though. We ain't do shit to nobody and they come shaking niggas up. They damn near choke slammed Brink's ass on the hood of the car. I wasn't having that shit, man," Peabo said, sitting down on the couch.

Peabo was like a younger brother to me and the closest to my heart. If there was anybody I would kill for other than Ma Dukes, it would be him. Ma Dukes took him in before she took me in.

Ma Dukes wasn't bullshitting when she said she was nosey. She's probably the nosiest person I know. She was like the project's watch dog. If she ain't got shit to do, she sits on her stool all day long and just watch everything and everybody and on top of that, she had a great memory.

She found Peabo sleeping inside of an abandoned van that sat in the back parking lot. Night after night, she would sit in the window and see Peabo going inside the van and wouldn't come out until the morning time. It was the night of a bad winter storm we had in 1999, when she felt bad for the kid and went outside to get him. It was cold, snowing and windy when she walked out there. She said she opened up the hatch of the van and he was balled up inside the spare tire compartment with a dingy sheet and some tarp. She brought him inside her home where she fed him and gave him a place to sleep. She woke up the next day and he was gone and so was her wallet. What he didn't know was that the money he had taken was just pocket change to Ma Dukes. She didn't care about him taking her money, what she cared about was the respect, so she went out to look for him. She found him a few days later. He had spent all the money and was back dumpster diving for food and sleeping in cars. Once again, she brought him back home with her and made him work to pay off the money he had stolen from her. Since then, he's been living here with her. I, on the other hand, had moved out after a while. Peabo was a momma's boy; he wasn't leaving the projects without Ma Dukes, and Ma Dukes was not leaving the projects at all. How else was she going to know what was going on?

Peabo and I actually put our money together and purchased Ma Dukes a house, but her hood booger ass went and rented it out. She was going to die in this apartment, right there in her window stool.

She picked up her purse, walked over to the window, and sat down on her stool. She opened her purse and pulled out her gun and tucked it back in her hiding spot behind the radiator.

"Ma, what you needed your gun for?" I asked her.

"The way they were out there tossing my baby around. I was about to catch a body. They already had him in the back of the car by the time I got down there though."

"You was about to body a cop, Ma Dukes?" Mars asked.

"Damn right."

"That's what's up. I can rock with you," Mars said to Ma Dukes.

"Yea, I'll kill Obama for them two right there." I got up off the couch and went to the refrigerator.

"Ma, you ain't cook nothing?" I asked, looking over at the stove.

"I sho' did not. What, you done worked yourself up an appetite before I came in?"

"What you talking about, old woman?" I asked, playing dumb. She looked over at me then lit her cigarette.

"Baby girl, I think you missing something," she said to Mars, pointing at something on the floor. Mars stood up to see what she was pointing at, and I looked over there too. It was Mars's panties.

"What makes you think those belong to her, Ma? How you know those ain't Lynea's?"

"Because they weren't there when I left out earlier, but they here now. And when I walked in, Miss missy had guilt written all over her face. It's cool though, as long as ya kept y'all nasty asses out my kitchen." I looked over at Mars and laughed. She started blushing.

MA DUKES

The kids sat here for a little while longer talking and watching TV while the whole time I couldn't help but to stare at Mars. She looked exactly like Jessica, when Jessica was clean, but those eyes were him. Those dark, black, sadistic eyes were all him. I had seen those eyes before on Ishmell, Trub's father. His eyes were naturally green but when he got mad his eyes turned dark as night and he became a whole other person that you didn't want to be around. Ishmell was always friendly with the ladies back in the day. Hell, I even had my chance with him, but that was between him and I.

Like I mentioned before, I'm a nosey ass motherfucker, so I knew who was fucking with whom and who did what around here. Somehow, Nancy always found out about them other women, but she never found out about us because him and I played the brother sister role pretty good. Ishmell was messing with Jessica heavy before she became known as Jessica Do It All. I even dropped him off at Jessica's mother house a few times. Nancy never found out about Jessica either because Jessica didn't live in these projects then. Jessica later moved in the back buildings after she had given birth to her daughter and was able to qualify for welfare and Section 8.

Once she moved to the projects, Ish stopped messing with her completely to prevent Nancy from finding out. I think he might have paid her off to keep her mouth shut about them. I couldn't believe I was staring his possible side kid in the face. Forget possible, this was indeed his kid; those eyes were two of a kind. *Shit, how was I going to tell Trub that he may have been sleeping with his sister,* I thought. I think I'll just leave this for Ishmell to handle. I don't think this was any of my business.

JAY

"Ah shit, baby girl. Ease up just a little," I yelled out in pain.

"I'm sorry, baby, my mind is elsewhere," Jamila said, as she continued to redress my wounds from when I was shot. Most of them were healing but I was still feeling soreness in some of the spots.

"Yea, I know, but it'll be ok. Still haven't heard anything from Venus?" I asked her.

"Nope, not yet, and her phone keeps going straight to voicemail. What happened to Lodi probably made her ass bug the fuck out. I wouldn't be surprise if her crazy alter ego is somewhere walking around proudly."

"What the hell is up with that shit?"

"With what, Venus?" she asked, as she kneeled down and started removing the bandage on my calf as I started rolling up.

"It's a disorder she had since she was younger. She had a rough childhood; she was the child of a crackhead. She basically took care of herself since the age of four. She went to school where she had no friends, and was constantly teased about how she looked and smelled. She wasn't loved by her mom and she had no friends, so what's a child to do? She created an imaginary friend who she named Mars. Eventually, Mars started becoming a part of her. If she had someone in her life that actually cared about her, they could have caught her condition sooner and maybe Venus wouldn't have been in certain predicaments that she's in. I met

Venus in juvi. I felt bad for her so I befriended her. She grew a trust for me and opened up about her mom selling her innocence for crack when she was 9 years old. She told me about Mars, in which I didn't believe her at first, until one day Venus's ass switched on me and I came face to face with this Mars person, who is indeed the opposite of Venus."

"Wow, that's some freaky ass shit," I responded with a laugh. I couldn't believe it because I had never seen the shit, but Loc told me he witnessed baby girl bug out at the club.

"It's not funny, the shit is real and it's spooky. Her fucking eyes go from Venus green to charcoal black in 2.5 seconds, and I don't scare easily, but that shit scared the hell out of me. But anyway, Venus finally told me that she was diagnosed with Dissociative Identity Disorder which is another form of Schizophrenia."

"Wait, so ma can become a whole other person or some shit?" I questioned.

"Yea, basically. Another person with a whole different personality and different life, and that exactly what Mars is, the opposite of Venus. Venus is sweet, Mars is a bitch. God versus Lucifer."

"You think that shit will ever go away?"

"I don't think so. When it comes to the mind, there's really no cure. She just has to know how to control the shit, I guess."

"Damn, ma is really fucked up in the head."

"Yea, but that's my psycho and I love her to death. I just hope she's alright," Jamila said, looking up at me.

"You have some beautiful eyes, you know that, bunny?" I said, cupping her chocolate brown face.

"So I've been told."

"Oh yea?"

"Yep, I was also told I have DSEs," she said.

"What the hell is DSEs?"

"Dick sucking eyes," she answered, causing me to laugh so hard I was in pain.

"Yo, I had never heard of that one. Come here, ma," I said, reaching out for her hands and pulling her up to her feet. I grabbed her by the back of her knees and pulled her down on to my lap so that she was now straddling me.

"You be sucking dick, bunny?"

"Not anymore," she answered.

"And why is that?"

"Because my new boo doesn't have one," she said, reaching down and kissing me on the lips.

"Who said I ain't have one? You know damn well I stay strapped. If you need me to pull Tyson out the closet, just say the word. I'll knock that pussy out like fight night."

"Don't make promises you can't keep, baby," Jamila said.

"You only talking shit right now because I'm hurt, but you know what it is. I'll bust that ass. Have you deep throating Tyson. Lay down. Matter of fact, turn that ass around and let me bite ya butt," I said, flipping her over on her stomach. I may have been hurt but I had a little strengthen left in me. I got between her legs and pulled her little booty shorts down off her butt, and her whole chocolate ass came bouncing out. Her cheeks looked like two oversized brownies. I gripped both cheeks and then bent down and started biting on them. I spread her cheeks and licked her ass crack, making her giggle.

"Stop, that tickles," she laughed. I brought my tongue from between her cheeks and up the small of her back, and up to her neck where I started biting her.

"Mmm, I like that," Jamila moaned.

"Oh yeah," I responded, as I put my finger in my mouth and then back down, sticking my finger in her already wet pussy.

"Damn, girl, why you so wet? You got ya own little chocolate lava going on down here," I said, as I pushed my fingers further into her and she let out a moan.

"I think you ready for Tyson, ma. Stay right here and don't move." I jumped out the bed and went to the closet just as my phone started ringing.

"Who the fuck is that?" I picked up the phone and looked at it. It was my mother so I answered it.

"Not right now, Ma, I'm busy."

"But Jayla, baby, I just wanted to see how you were doing?"

"Ma, I'm good, I'm going to call you right back," I said, hanging up the phone and placing it back on the dresser. I reached to the top of the closet and grabbed Tyson and was on my way to the bed when my phone started ringing again. I walked over and picked it up.

"Ma, I said I'm going to call you back," I answered the phone without looking at the caller ID.

"Yo, it's me," Loc shouted in the phone.

"My bad, dog, I thought you was Ma calling. Is this important? If not, I'm gonna have to get back at you."

"Yea, Lodi is up, he's trying to talk. They're removing his breathing tube now. You might want to give Ma a call back," Loc said.

"I'm on my way," I said before hanging up the phone.

LODI

"What up, Loc?" I whispered, as I took a sip of water because my throat was dry and sore from the breathing tube.

"I'm good, bro. I'm happy to be looking at yo' ugly, black ass face," Loc joked. I tried laughing but it was too painful.

"I'm not even going to respond to your stupidity. How long have I been in here?" I asked, my voice a little louder than before, thanks to the water.

"About three, maybe four weeks now. What the fuck happened, dude?" Loc asked.

"Man, I faintly remember. All I remember is Venus and I leaving out the building and we were crossing the street where I had parked my car. How ironic is it that the one day I park on the street instead of the garage, my ass gets run down? Somebody had to be watching my ass. I'll put all my money on that nigga, Trub. The moment I'm able to walk, I'm running up on that nigga and slicing his throat."

"Nigga, you ain't about that life. Leave the gully shit to me. What makes you think it was him?"

"That nigga ain't get his street fame from being dumb. He's a smart nigga so I'm sure he figured out it was us who sprayed up the 'jects and not to mention, the nigga had a thing for Venus, or Mars, shall I say. He probably was more so watching her than me. Speaking of her, where is V?" I asked Loc. He looked at me and shrugged his shoulders.

"What the hell you mean?" I asked, imitating his shoulder shrug.

"Nobody seen her since you got hit."

"What you mean? She was right there when it happened?"

"Yea, well she may have been there when you got popped, but she wasn't in the hospital when they brought you here, and she hasn't been back to the house and she's not answering her cell phone," Loc said.

"Have y'all checked with that nigga Trub? If it was him who ran me down, then it's a possibility that Venus may be with him. I need to get out this hospital and find my baby girl."

"Nigga, where the hell you going with a fractured femur, a displaced hip and three broken ribs?" Loc asked.

"I been lying up in this hospital for how long and this shit ain't heal yet?" Loc just sat there looking at me like I was stupid.

"Exactly, nigga. All ya ashy ass been doing is lying up in the hospital, nigga. You know you need to be exercising that shit on the regular."

"Yo, you still got that crazy physical therapist chick number?" I asked.

"My name is Joann, not crazy physical therapist chick. Careful how you speak to me, Ladonis; your walking future is in my hands now," a cute older woman came inside the room carrying bags. She looked to be in her mid-40s. She looked like Pam Grier when she played Foxy Brown. I looked at Loc who couldn't tear his eyes away from her ass, until she turned around to place her bags on the floor. Now I was able to see why he couldn't help but stare. Ms. Ma'am was stacked. I was going to joke with Loc about him messing with an older woman, but she was a cougar.

"Look, Joann, I'm willing to pay whatever it is you want if you can get me to walk again in the least time possible. I have business I need to handle."

"Well, Ladonis, I can't promise you a miracle just yet. Your doctor hasn't cleared you for the maximum therapy, but give me two weeks and a few grand, and I'll get you there," she said with a charming smile.

"You got it. Where we starting?" I asked. She picked up my x-rays and held them up towards the light for a few seconds, then placed it back inside the folder. She picked up my chart and started reading as she walked over to me.

"Well, first we have to work that neck out. If you can't hold ya neck up then this therapy is useless," she said, placing my chart on the bed and reaching behind me and holding my head up so that my head and neck were aligned. She started removing my neck brace gently.

"Ok, now Ladonis, I need you to slowly try and lift your neck out of my hand." I never realized how heavy my head was until this moment. I attempted to lift my head but it wasn't going anywhere. It felt like my head weighed a ton.

"Don't strain now. I don't need you busting a blood vessel. Just let it come naturally." I rested my head back in her hands and when I felt like I was ready, I attempted to lift my head but nothing.

"It's ok, this is just day one. Even when I'm not here, Ladonis, you need to practice. I promise I'll have you up and moving soon," she said, wrapping the brace back around my neck and placing my head back on the pillow. She walked over and picked up her bags.

"See you tomorrow," she said, walking over to Loc and handing him a card.

"What's this?" he asked.

"My address. My husband goes to work at eight. You still have my number, give me a call." He shook his head up and down and placed the number inside his pocket. She walked out the room, shutting the door behind her.

"So ya ass wasn't going to share the fact the you were messing with someone almost twice ya age, nigga?"

"Shut ya ass up. I'm about to get going," Loc said, getting up and coming over to give me a pound.

"Where you going? After grandma?"

"And you know this, man," he said, smiling from ear to ear before jogging out the room.

MARS

"So foot on the brake, hands at nine and two; make sure you can see out of your mirrors and put ya seat belt on. Now with ya foot on the brake, move the gear shift into drive and slowly lift your foot off the brake and just let the car glide," Trub said from the passenger side of the car. He had borrowed one of his boy's beat up piece of shit of a car to teach me how to drive. I did as he said, slowly releasing the brake.

"Ok, good. Now give it a little gas."

"Why couldn't I learn in your car?" I asked, as I pressed down on the gas and the car took off, causing my head to hit the back of the seat.

"Oh shit," he said as he leaned down and used his hand to press on the brake.

"This is why yo' ass can't drive my car. Put this shit in park. Today's lesson is over."

"But why? I was just getting the hang of it."

"No you weren't. Yo' ass was trying to kill us, that's what you were doing. I think you need a professional to teach you how to drive. I'll find you a driving school, let you kill them. Get out the driver's seat, Mars," Trub said, coming around to my side of the car.

"This is so messed up. How we gon' be Bonnie and Clyde if you won't teach me how to drive?" I asked, now pouting and getting out the car.

"We can be the non-driving version of them, baby luv. Come on, let's be out," he said as we both got in the car and he pulled off.

"Where we headed?" I asked.

"I have to handle something," he responded, lighting up a blunt.

"Something like what?" I asked, looking down at the hair hanging from my head. I needed something done to it immediately.

"Something ya spooky ass might enjoy."

"Cool," I said, sitting back in the seat and enjoying the ride.

We ended up in some abandoned factory on the side of the Hudson River.

When we pulled up, I noticed Trub's Benz sitting in front of the building. We pulled up next to it. Mikey came walking up to the car and opened my door for me to get out.

"Yo, give me my shit back. I can't get with all this high-class technology going on in this shit," Mikey said, kicking the tire of Trub's Benz.

"Kick my car again, I'll have baby girl body ya ass," Trub said, giving Mikey back the keys to his little beat up Honda.

We walked inside the factory and I could hear someone in there screaming. When we got in the huge room, there was a guy tied up to iron pegs that were embedded in the floor of the warehouse. I immediately became intrigued.

"What's going on here?" I asked, circling the man tied to the floor.

"Ol' Romey Rome here, has a debt with Ma Dukes that's past due. When Ma asked him for her money, he told her to suck his dick," Trub explained.

"And I don't take to well to disrespect," I heard Ma Dukes voice come from out the crowd.

"Hey, baby," she said kissing Trub on the cheek.

"So what do you plan on doing with him?" I asked, looking down at the wiggling, screaming man.

"Help, help!" he yelled to the top of his lungs.

"Shut the fuck up, no one can hear yo' ass. I don't know. Ma, what you wanna do to him?" Trub questioned Ma Dukes.

"I think this nigga could use a bath," Ma Dukes said, taking a puff of her cigarette.

"A bath? The hell you care about his hygiene for, this nigga ain't leaving out of here alive," I said.

"Oh, trust me baby girl, this ain't no regular bath." I looked over at Ma Dukes and then walked over to Trub, digging in his pocket, and for some reason, everyone in the room ducked. I looked around confused as I held up the knife I had just retrieved.

"It's just a knife y'all, damn, chill out. I ain't shooting no one today," I said to them.

"Damn, baby luv, you got my niggas scared of that trigger finger of yours," Trub joked with me.

"I see," I said, walking over to the yelling captive. I opened the knife as I sat down on his chest. He started wiggling and bucking, trying to throw me off him. I grabbed on to his mouth and tried to pry it open, but it wasn't budging.

"Yo, you, come over here," I called to one of Trub's boys that was standing around watching. I had met him before, but there were so many of them that I couldn't keep up with the names.

"Who, me?" he asked.

"Yeah, you." He slowly walked over to me.

"Hold his mouth open and if he bites me, I'll kill you," I said, looking him in his eyes. He hesitantly bent down and grabbed on to his face, then opened the guy's mouth and held it open with all his strength. I grabbed the guy's tongue and with the knife, I sliced through the flesh of his tongue. The knife slid through his tongue like it was butter. The guy, no longer able to scream for help, cried out in pain as I detached his tongue from his mouth.

"Ah shit," the guy that was holding the mouth open for me said, as he let the guy go and ran out the warehouse gagging.

With the severed tongue in my hand, I walked over to Ma Dukes, grabbed her hand and placed the tongue in her hand.

"Let's see how he uses that tongue to disrespect you again."

"You're something else, little girl," Ma Dukes said, looking at me, stunned at what I had just done. I smiled at her because she didn't know half of the shit that went on in my demented brain.

"What ideas do you have in that pretty little mind of yours to get rid of this scum?" Ma Dukes asked.

"Anyone know where I could get some acid and a torch from?" I asked.

****

Two hours later, we were pulling up to the projects. I had just had the time of my life back at the warehouse, as I watched the flesh melt off that the dude's bone. Some of the guys couldn't stomach the sight, so they all scattered one by one until it was just myself and Ma Dukes left inside the room. When I was done, they came back into the warehouse and dragged the charred bones to the river edge and tossed them in.

"I have blood on my clothes," I said to Trub as he put the car in park.

"Don't worry, baby girl, I'll take you shopping for some new clothes," Trub said.

"Well, if I knew how to drive, I wouldn't have to depend on you to take me shopping. Or I could have just gone to get some of Venus's clothes. That dude Lodi really hooked her wardrobe up."

"You don't need any clothes another nigga bought. I got you, ma, just give me a minute."

"Speaking of him, have you heard anything about his condition?" I asked Trub.

"Nope."

"You should have just deaded that nigga that day. You know if he survives, he's coming for Venus, and that's all she needs is to show her face again and it's lights out for my ass."

"You'll be cool, ma, don't worry about him," Trub said.

"So you say. What you need to do is go up there and finish his ass," I said, getting out the car and walking towards the building. When we got there, Peabo was standing there hugged up on some girl. I couldn't really see who she was until she turned around and we made eye contact.

"What's up, Peabo? How you doing, Lynea?" Trub said, giving Peabo dap and then the girl Lynea a hug. I don't know what it was about this girl, but those eyes were so haunting. Where did I know her from?

"Lynea, this my baby luv here, Mars."

"Hey," she said in a low voice and a half ass wave. She was a really pretty brown-skinned girl. She had the brightest brown doe eyes, curly shoulder length hair, and plump lips. She was petite with long legs, wide hips, and I could tell by looking, home girl had a bumper on her. I couldn't be sure because she was sitting on Peabo's lap.

"What's up?" I responded to them both.

"What y'all about to get in to?" Peabo asked Trub.

"I just need to go talk to Ma Dukes for a minute and then baby girl needs to go shopping."

"Well, Lynea was about to shoot to the mall, why don't you tag along with her?" Peabo asked me.

"No, I'm alright," I said, shaking my head. I didn't know this girl and I was not about to get in the car with her.

"Yea, go head, baby luv. Here," Trub said, reaching in his pocket and pulling out a knot of money. He peeled off half the stack and handed it to me.

"I don't mind. I don't like going to the mall by myself anyway," the girl Lynea said with a smile. I was suspicious about the girl but the only way to find out more about her was to get to know her.

"Ok, cool, let's go," I said to her.

"See you later, baby."

JAMILA

"Come on, babe, I don't want to miss the 7 for 27 deal at Victoria Secrets," I begged Jay who was walking slower than my dead grandma. It's been over two months since she's been shot and she's still trying to play the hurt card, but I wasn't falling for the shit. All she wanted to do was sit in the house and have me baby her ass all damn day.

"What the hell is a 7 for 27 deal anyway?" she asked as she dragged her feet.

"I can get 7 panties for 27 dollars," I shrieked while jumping up and down.

"Wow, how exciting," she said sarcastically.

"Well, since you don't think it's a big deal, don't be looking forward to seeing me in them. I'm going to make sure whenever I come by, I got my period panties on."

"Yea, ok, I'm kicking ya ass right back out my house. You ain't see that sign that's on my bedroom door?" she asked.

"What sign?"

"The No Granny Panties Allowed. Lace Only sign," she responded. I laughed.

"You so stupid. Well, you just take ya time and meet me in the store, crippled ass," I said, as I fast walked toward the store. I already saw a crowd of women heading towards the store so I picked up my pace to a little jog so that I wouldn't miss out on the good panties.

As soon as I got in there, there were women surrounding the panties shelves just ruffling through. I made my way up to the front and was right along with them, looking for my size. It took me a while because the sizes were now mixed up, but I was able to track down six pairs that I liked that were my size. I spotted some black laced boy short that I had to have and I prayed they were my size. I reached for them at the same time someone else was reaching for them.

"Excuse me, I seen these first," I said to the other woman.

"No, I had them in my hand first when you reached and grabbed them," she responded. This bitch must ain't know who she was talking to. My ass fights dirty and I was 10 seconds from strangling her ass with a thong if she ain't let my panties go.

"Well, I have them in my hand now and I ain't letting them go. We can stand here all damn day, bitch."

"I ain't got shit to do," the boney bitch said.

"Well I do," somebody said from the crowd. I recognized that voice which made me lose focus of what I was doing. I looked her dead in her eyes and already knew.

"How the fuck did I know yo' ass was out here running around?"

"I see you finally learned to tell the difference between us. What, you missing your little friend?"

"As a matter of fact, I do. Only the devil knows what ya sadistic ass been up to, probably got my friend into all kinds of shit."

"Well, guess what? She's long gone, bitch. I'm here now and I ain't going anywhere," Mars said, staring at me with those sinister eyes.

"We'll see, bitch," I smiled.

"I hope you picked out something sexy for me to take off you," Jay said, finally making her crippled ass to the store and walking up behind me. When I didn't respond back to her, she turned and looked at who I was giving my death stare to.

"Yo Venus, we been looking all over for ya ass, where you been?" Mars never responded, she just kept staring me down.

"That ain't Venus, baby. Let's just go," I said, pulling Jay in the other direction.

"Bye, bitch. Give Lodi a kiss for me. Tell him Venus and I both miss those juicy pink lips of his." I rolled my eyes, turned, and proceeded to walk out the door. That was until the alarm went off. I turned and looked and remember the six pairs of panties in my hand. I threw them on one of the shelves and we kept on walking out the store.

"I hate that bitch. I would really enjoy running that bitch over."

"Yea, well you can't do that. At least I can bring some good news to my brother. That nigga stressing himself out worried about her."

"Alright, well can we just follow them? I need to be sure that she's really ok," I said to Jay.

"If that'll make you happy, bunny, sure," Jay said.

"You're so sweet, baby. Come on," I said, pulling on Jay's

arm.

"Ah shit, bunny," she screamed.

"I'm sorry, baby," I apologized. I had completely forgotten that was her bad arm.

MARS

"I think I'm about finished, how about you?" I asked Lynea, who still seemed to be looking for more shit to buy. I already had both arms full of clothes and not to mention, the clothes that I had already purchased.

"Uh, yep, we can go now," she said, picking up a royal blue tank top and throwing it on to her pile of clothes.

"Yo' ass can shop. I don't know how you do it, I ain't got the patience for the shit." We had been in this mall for over two hours already and I was ready to get far away from here as possible. We got up to the register to pay for all of our items. It seemed like it took another hour just to ring up all of our stuff. I was relieved once our asses were out of that damn store.

"I just need to stop at one more store. I need a pair of shoes to wear to the boat party tonight," Lynea said.

"You have three pair already, girl," I said to her.

"I know, but these won't make bitches break their necks. I need some fly shits for when I step up on that boat. Are you coming? I think I heard Peabo say Trub was going."

"Uh, I don't know. I'm not much of a party person. I would rather just kick it in the house."

"That sucks. You're going to miss out on so much fun and an open bar and fireworks."

"I'm sure I'll be fine. Where are you from?" I asked her. I really couldn't get over those eyes of hers, I just couldn't remember where I knew her from.

"I'm from here originally, but I moved to North Carolina with my family. Once I got old enough, I brought my ass right back up here. I'm a Jersey girl for life, see," she said, turning around and lifting her shirt up, showing me her tattoo. She had a tattoo going down the spine of her back that read Jersey with a crown on the letter J.

"Nice."

"Where are you from?" she asked me.

"I'm from here for the most part, not really too sure where exactly. My mother was a crackhead and I never knew my father. I was in Edna for most of my life.

"Edna, the correctional facility?" she asked.

"Yep," I answered. I turned and looked at her to see if I may have freighted her, but she seemed to have a smile on her face.

"The hell you smiling for?" I asked her.

"Nothing. Let's go in here," she said, pulling me into Saks.

"So where are ya parents?" I asked her as she tried on a pair of shoes.

"Don't have any. They died when I was young."

"Oh. How did you meet Peabo?"

"Uhhh, I used to work with them before they started turning drugs. When they were just stick-up kids, I would play the decoy who would distract the target while they did what they had to do."

"So you were putting yourself at risk for them?"

"You can say that, but it all paid off. Ma Dukes was paying me lovely and on top of that, Trub was hitting me off every now and then," she said with a smile.

"What you mean hitting you off every now and then? Hitting you off with what?" I asked her.

"Dick. What you think about these shoes?" she asked, standing up and posing in the shoes, waiting on my opinion.

"Cute. So what you're telling me is that you were fucking Trub and now you fucking Peabo?"

"Exactly, but me and Trub was more so out of boredom. I wasn't feeling him but he damn sure knew how to lay that pipe, girl. I'm sure you know this. Peabo on the other hand, I actually like him. He's not a dick like ya man. He's kind. When Ma Dukes took me in a few years back, Peabo took me shopping, kept my pockets loaded, but it was too much. I wanted to make my own money and I did. I made enough and I moved out the 'jects. I wanted Peabo to come with me but he was not leaving Ma Dukes; she's his world. If anything happened to that woman, hell will rise in New Jersey," Lynea said, looking over at me, as I stood there with my arms folded across my chest, still trying to get the fact that she slept with both Peabo and Trub.

"Don't worry about me and Trub, I promise you it was the past."

"Oh, I wasn't worried about that. He knows where it's at and he knows I'm a crazy individual, so he knows not to play me."

"Cool. So what you think about these?" she asked, posing in the shoes.

"Cute, now let's be out." She picked up both pairs of shoes, brought them to the counter and paid for them, and then we finally left out the damn mall.

We were driving down the highway, cruising and listening to music, when I noticed a car that had been behind us since we left the mall.

"Lynea, make a right," I demanded to her.

"A right? Where you trying to go, chick?"

"I think we're being followed."

"Oh yea, we are. I peeped them as we were leaving the mall's parking garage. You probably thought I got lost in parking garage but I didn't. I was making my own circle. I been working with Ma Dukes, Trub and Peabo way too long to be caught slipping. I was just going to lead their ass back to the projects."

"I doubt if they're dumb enough to follow us back to the projects."

"Those the two chicks from earlier?" she asked.

"I think so."

"Here," she said, reaching in her pocketbook and pulling out a gun.

"I hope you know how to use this."

"I've held a few of Trub's," I said, looking over the beautiful piece in my hand.

"I'm going to go down a dead end and if they still following, start blasting," she said. I shook my head up and down, never giving her eye contact. She maneuvered her way through the blocks like she knew exactly where she was going. She was driving for about five minutes before she made a left on Getty Avenue and drove until we couldn't drive anymore. The car was a few feet away from us. With a smile on my face, I cocked the gun and was ready to get it popping. My trigger finger was itching and the killer in me was jumping up and down. That was until the car turned inside of the Planet Fitness parking lot, crushing my hopes.

"They must've knew we were on to them, dumb bitches. Let's get out of here," Lynea said.

"Fuck that, let's go after their asses," I responded.

"Bitch, you out of ya mind. Trub ain't choking me out for taking you on a killing spree. Pump ya brakes, ma," Lynea said, reaching over and trying to take her gun from me, but I wasn't letting it go. *Where the hell did I know this girl from*? I thought as I looked her in her eyes as she reached over for the gun. I let the gun go and she placed it back inside her purse and pulled off.

When we got back to the projects, all the guys were kicking it in front of the building.

"Hey, baby luv, how was shopping?" Trub asked. He was sitting on a milk crate in front of the building drinking a V8 carrot juice.

"It was cool. I ran into Venus's little black ass friend and her carpet munching girlfriend. How do you drink that nasty shit?"

"Word? That dike ain't dead? I thought we murdered her ass, and this ain't nasty. Huh, try it," he said, putting it to my lips, but I smacked it out his hand and he smacked me on the butt.

"Nope, and neither is Lodi. How you get the name ruthless and y'all can't knock off one nigga and a wannabe nigga. I guess I got to do the shit myself," I muttered, as I started picking at my nails. I heard one of Trub's boys laugh which caused me to look up at him.

"What the fuck is so funny?" I questioned.

"Leave the killing to the dicks, aight, ma," he said, grabbing on his crotch area of his pants.

"Ya disrespectful ass wanna die today or tomorrow?" I asked him.

"Uh, maybe next week, I have shit to do tomorrow," his smart ass answered. He must've thought I was playing, but I was dead serious. He really ain't know who he was fucking with.

"I'll remember that," I said, focusing my attention back on my nails.

"Stop that," Trub demanded, smacking my hand from my mouth.

"Stop what?"

"Biting ya shits. Why you just don't go get them done? Fingers look like you been working on the railroad or some shit."

"You wasn't complaining when they were wrapped around ya dick last night, were you?" I turned around and cooed in his ear. He wrapped his arm around my waist.

"I don't mind them shits, but clearly you do. You can't keep them out ya mouth," he said, smacking my fingers again.

"Watch yourself, Najavar. You don't want to wake up missing fingers," Ma Dukes shouted from the window.

"That's right, Ma, let him know," I said.

"I ain't worried about the psycho, I got her kryptonite in my back pocket," Trub said.

"The hell you talking about?" I asked him. He reached in his pocket and pulled out a bottle of pills. I recognized the little blue pills and immediately tried reaching for them.

"Nope, get yo' ass out of here," Trub said, putting the bottle behind his back.

"Where did you get those?" I asked him, jumping off his lap and running behind him to get the pills, but he had brought them back to the front of him.

"Out ya pocketbook. I thought I told you to flush these shits?"

I jumped on his back and playfully attempted to put him in a headlock, but he lowered his chin so I couldn't get a good grip. He stood up with me on his back.

"Say I won't back into this wall." I reached down in the back of his pants and pulled out his gun.

"I dare you."

"Alright, you got it, ma," he laughed, with his hands up.

"Like I thought," I said, snatching the pills out his hand and jumping down off his back.

"Little violent, sexy ass," he said, slapping me on the butt and taking his gun out my hand and placing it back in his pants.

"You ready to be out?"

"Yea, I'm tired, I need a nap."

"You always need a nap, ya sleepy ass. Come on, let's get ya bags." We turned and started walking towards the car. I looked back because I had the feeling someone was watching me and I was right. The Lynea chick was staring me down with the coldest look on her face. It wasn't that warm look like earlier, it was more of hatred. This chick had a secret grudge against me. I could feel it just by the way she was looking at me just now.

"Tell me about this chick Lynea that you sent me off with," I insisted, as I started removing the bags and handing them to him. Something wasn't right about this chick and I was determined to figure the shit out.

TRUB

Later That Night...

I stepped on the boat looking good as hell in my Tom Ford, fitted, black button up, a pair of black Armani Exchange jeans, and my black Jordan Masters. I had my black New York fitted pulled low over my eyes and a prize on my arm. Mars had on a killer little black dress, and by killer, I mean killer. I damn near swallowed my tongue when she stepped out the room. The little black dress was fitted to her body perfectly with cutouts that showed just enough skin. Her hair had this wet style going on, like she had washed her hair and just let it air dry. All of her assets sat up so perfectly in that dress. That was until I peeled her ass out of that shit and had her climbing the bedroom walls. I would have still been in that ass if she had not gotten sick suddenly. She had to throw up, so I had to let her down off the wall so she could run to the bathroom. I guess it was something she ate. I tried to convince her to stay home tonight but she wasn't having that shit. She threw up at least two more times before we left out the door. I told her ass if she threw up in my car I was putting her out on the side of the road. Of course, she threatened to stab me.

When we got on the boat, it seemed like the whole hood was in this bitch. It was packed as hell. If Christie wanted to get rid of all the black folks in Jersey, all he had to do was sink this damn boat because it was like Black People Meet up in this bitch. I held Mars close to me as we made our way through the crowd. Peabo had already texted me and told me him, Lynea and Mike was here, it was just the trouble of finding their asses now.

About five minutes of walking through the crowd, we finally found them on the top deck.

"How yo' ass manage to get a VIP section, nigga?" I asked Peabo, giving him and Mikey dap and hugging Lynea.

"Money talks, bro. You gotta give them what they want to get what you want. I paid some chick double what she paid to get this shit. It was only her and two of her girls occupying the big ass area.

"Hey, Mars, you look cute," Lynea complimented Mars.

"I know," Mars said, giving her a look and a fake ass smile. I laughed. Mars was something else. She all of a sudden didn't like Lynea. I thought maybe it was the fact that she found out about Lynea and I messing around back then, but for the two months Mars has been with me, I never took her as the type of chick to get mad over shit like that. Me fucking with Lynea was out of boredom, so it doesn't bother me that she's with P now. Now, I consider her like my sister. In some way she is. She's one of Ma Dukes' strays.

I've known Lynea for some years now and she's never rubbed me the wrong way, and usually I can sense when something isn't right. Lynea has helped us make a shit load of money. Just like Peabo and I, she felt indebted to Ma Dukes, so when Ma Dukes brought the idea of her helping us stick niggas up, she was all for it. She never asked for anything in return, but of course we made sure to keep her pockets and bank accounts stacked. Since we transitioned to the drug game, we haven't really had a need for her as much. Drug game was a man's game. The only time we involved her in the game was when we robbed Lodi's trap.

Doing what she does best, Lynea was able to slip right in past Lodi's pussy ass bodyguard nigga. All she did was put a little more switch in her ass and put on some lip gloss, and she had the nigga right where she needed him. Same thing with the door man. She faked like she was lost and had the wrong apartment. When the nigga got a look of her, his dumb ass opened the door and let her right in. She put his ass down and two other niggas that was in there. Shorty was nice with the banger. So nice, I went and copped her a custom pink gun set that came with a glock, a Ruger and an AK. I didn't know too much about Lynea, just that her parents were killed when she was eight. She didn't live too far from the projects when it happened. She said she was in the house when it happened, and all she remembers was a little girl in her house and then fire.

"Yo, where Seth and SP at, I thought them niggas was here too?"

"They are, they down there on the dance floor. You know them two pervs don't waste no time." I shook my head.

"Let me go holla at them niggas. You alright, baby luv?"

"Yea, I think so. Can you bring me a water when you come back?"

"Aight," I said, kissing her on her forehead before I left. When

I got down to the lower level of the boat, there were people everywhere. It felt like a club. The vibe was smooth as hell. No one was on their bullshit. On the way down there, I realized I knew almost everyone here, and everyone knew me. From the niggas to the bitches, my name was getting called in every direction. Some of my smash and go hoes were in here, too, trying to hug up on me, but if they only knew about my crazy ass shawty upstairs, they would back the fuck up.

"White boy," I said walking up to Seth. I called him white boy because he was Albino. That shit still ain't stop the ladies from fighting over his ass. He used to be one of my main niggas who didn't think twice before blasting a nigga. His trigger finger was loose as hell. He gave up the stick up life when his seed was born. I don't blame him.

"Field Boy," he responded giving me dap.

"How's my god baby?"

"She's good, getting big as shit. I think it's time for me to dust off the Ruger. I know how these fast ass little niggas think."

"My nigga, she's two. If a little nigga chasing after her it's because she took his cheese doodle or something. You got a little bit more time to go before we both be hanging little niggas up on the electricity wires by their shoe strings."

"That's why you my nigga and her god father. How Ma Dukes?" he asked.

"You know her, she's always ok. She mad at ya ass anyway. You haven't brought Breanna to see her yet."

"I know. I tried once, but she wasn't home."

"You tried once? Breanna is going on two and Ma still ain't seen her yet. But you know what, I'm gonna mind my business. Just be looking out for that right jab when you do go and see her. Where's SP?"

"His no rhythm ass over there dancing on somebody's daughter," Seth said, pointing in the direction of SP. I laughed at the sight of him dancing off beat behind some chick. It was hysterical. I walked up behind him and plucked him on the ear which made him turn around.

"Oh shit, what's up, Trub?" he said, giving me pound while still attempting to grind up against the girl's ass.

"Definitely not your rhythm, nigga. You better keep up with that ass," I boasted.

"What, nigga? Watch this," he said, as he started dancing a little harder trying to keep up with the chick. He even dropped it low right along with her. This had to be the funniest shit I had ever seen in my life. I decided to leave him alone and let him focus on his dancing, so I made my way back over to Seth.

"You need to teach ya boy some moves. Let me go over here and get shawty her water. I'll see y'all niggas back up in VIP," I said, walking over to get Mars's water and head back to the VIP section. I was almost up the stairs that were just below the VIP section, when I felt someone grab my hand like a nigga would do to get a chick's attention. I turned around and there was Marcia, this Jamaican chick I hit a few times before hooking up with Mars.

"What's up, Marcia?" I said, giving her a friendly hug. She tried to kiss me but I moved out the way.

"What's good, T, it's like that now?"

"How you been?" I asked her, completely ignoring her question.

"Horny without you, T. You already know the deal."

"Yea, I know, with ya fresh ass. You good though?" I asked her.

"No, I miss you, baby," she said, right before cold water and ice came down on top of her head, followed by the bucket. I jumped back just in time.

"That'll cool ya hot ass down," Mars said, standing there with her hands on her hips and a scowl on her face.

"What the fuck you do that for?" Marcia asked, now drenched in water.

"Don't ask me no questions, trick. Get gone before I toss yo' ass head first in the ocean."

"Bitch, you must be tripping, you don't know me," Marcia said taking out a switch blade.

"What, you gonna stab me?" Mars said with a smile on her face. Marcia was about to make her way up the step when I grabbed her and brought her back down the steps.

"Wrong move, baby girl."

"Nah, babe, let her ass up here," Mars insisted.

"Go dry yourself off, ma," I said to Marcia.

"Babe? That's what this is about? Let me tell you something, sweetheart. He may be ya babe now, but later he'll be just another dog ass nigga and you'll be just another hoe like the rest of us. He was babe to me just a few weeks ago. It's only a matter of time before you become just another bitch's name he can cross off his hit list."

"Man, shut ya ass up, you knew what it was before I fucked you. A smash and go, no feelings involved. Get yo' ass the fuck outta here, Marcia."

"Fuck you, Trub, and your whore too," Marcia said, walking away. I shook my head and went over to Mars.

"If that bitch don't make it off this boat alive, remember it's your fault," Mars said walking back to the chair. I followed her and sat down next to her.

"Did you have to throw that cold ass water on her?"

"She lucky that's all I did. Can I have my water please?" she asked, and I handed her the bottle of water. I reached over and tried to kiss her, but she put her hand up, causing me to kiss the palm of her hand.

MARS

"You want to come dance with me, baby luv?"

"Nope, I don't dance."

"Come on, T. You can come dance with me since ya brother act like he doesn't want to dance," Lynea said, standing up with her tight one-piece short set. That bitch must've bumped her damn head if she thought I was about to be okay with her dancing with my man.

"No, he's good. Come on, baby," I said, grabbing Trub's hand and walking him down the steps. I turned back around and looked at Lynea, who was standing there mean mugging me. If looks could kill, that bitch would be getting the electric chair, because she just murdered me and everyone I knew with that look.

"Well, I'm coming with y'all. I hope you don't mind," she said, walking down the stairs. I rolled my eyes and pulled Trub faster along.

When we got down to the dance floor, Tyga's song "Hookah" was on. Trub grabbed a hold of my waist as he walked me to the middle of the dance floor, and started grinding on my butt. I matched his grind and the music, as I pushed my ass up against his pelvis. I wasn't much of a dancer, but I figured it was just like sex, just with clothes on and to a faster rhythm. As we were dancing, I felt someone backing up against us. I looked behind Trub and that heffa Lynea was back throwing her butt against Trub. I spun Trub around so that I was now dancing where he was. When Lynea ain't feel that hard body anymore, she turned around and sucked her teeth when she saw my back. I guess she got mad because when I turned around, she was pulling some guy off the bar and started dancing with him. She was trying to have a dance battle because she was dancing hard with this other guy. After a while, I stopped paying her attention because she was showing me that my dancing was amateur compared to hers, but Trub was helping me out a lot. He was a great dancer. I have to remember to ask him how he learned to dance like this.

Twenty minutes later, I was tired and hot as hell. Trub went to the bar to get us something to drink as I stepped out to the deck to catch some of that ocean breeze. I started walking around the deck looking at the full view of the skyline from afar. I closed my eyes, trying to listen to the waves, but my attention was diverted when I heard someone mention Trub's name. I opened my eyes and looked over at the chick who I had dumped the ice bucket on. Her back was turned towards me as she leaned on the railing. Every now and then, she would step on the lower railing. The evil wheels in my head started spinning. There were people around but they weren't paying any attention to me. I hid in the shadows of the building, waiting for the perfect time. There was a boom and then a pop sound that I thought was from a gun, but then the sky lit up with beautiful colors. I found myself so mesmerized with the colors that I had to snap myself out of it and remember the task at hand. I checked my surrounds and now everyone's focus was on the sky, and so was the girl's, Marcia. I ran up behind her, pushed her so hard her head snapped back, right before her body went over the railing. I ran back into the shadow as I heard a slight splash.

"Bye, bitch," I said, just as there was another loud explosion in the sky.

"Here you go, baby," Trub said, handing me a glass of champagne.

"Thanks, baby." I kissed him on the lips and turned around towards the ocean, as he wrapped his arms around my waist and we sat there watching the fireworks.

MARS

1 Week Later

"Nigga, you heard they finally found Marcia's body. Shit was floating in the Hudson. They think she got drunk and fell over the railing," Peabo said, leaning into the car and talking to Trub. I sat there picking at my nails like I wasn't paying attention to the conversation.

"That's odd, because the last I checked, Marcia didn't drink," Trub responded, and I felt him look over at me. I know he knew I had something to do with what happened to her, but at this point I really didn't care. I felt nothing about what I did. No remorse, no guilt; in fact, I felt like she deserved it. She should have known not to talk shit to someone she didn't know. Especially if you just got caught trying to push up on their man, ole thirsty hoe. Oh well, I hope that river water quenched her thirst.

"Yea, they said they're still investigating so we'll see. Maybe someone pushed her in by mistake. They want to interview anyone she may have come into contact with that night and are reviewing the video footage from that night. Keep ya eyes out, sis. They might come and talk to you about that whole thing with the ice bucket," he said to me. I didn't respond, just continued to pick my nails.

"Aight, bro, we got to go. I'll catch you later," Trub said, giving him a pound. We were on our way to see Dr. Burke. I had missed my visit last week and he had been leaving voicemails on

Venus's phone, saying how her missing her appointments was not a part of the terms of her release. That she may be required to go back to Edna if she doesn't come this week, so here we were.

The car ride there was quiet. I guess he was expecting me to say something because he kept looking in my direction.

"Why you keep looking over here? You trying to make us crash or something?"

"Tell me the truth, Mars. Did you push that girl off the boat?" he asked me.

"I don't know what you're talking about," I answered.

"Seriously, Mars. Don't play me out, ma." I turned and looked up at him without saying a word. He looked at me then back at the road, then back at me again and shook his head.

"That girl ain't deserve that shit, ma. That's fucked up. I think the killer in you is sexy and all, but that shit ain't cool. Marcia didn't deserve that."

"You taking up for that bitch now?"

"Nah, I'm not, but it's just messed up. You know they say drowning and being burned alive is one of the worst ways to go? You think she deserved to suffer like that?"

"I damn sure do. You come out ya mouth wrong to me and I'll find a way for you not to ever use that mouth again," I said, now with my attention focused on him. He shook his head and continued to focus back on the road.

"Pull over," I said.

"Why?"

"Because, just pull over," I said again with my hand on the door handle. He pulled the car over to the side of the road. I opened the door and held my head out and started throwing up.

"What the fuck is wrong with me?" I asked, as I brought my head back inside of the car and shut the door.

"Are you pregnant?" he asked me.

"No!"

"How you know? We thought it was just something you ate last week, but what if it's not?" he asked.

"You bugging, I ain't pregnant. Let's just get going before Dr. Burke starts calling this phone again." After a few seconds of him staring at me, he put the car in drive and pulled off.

We arrived at Dr. Burke's office and I jumped out.

"I'll try and make this shit quick," I said, getting out the car and walking towards the building.

"Venus!" The overexcited receptionist said, jumping from her desk like always. Her happiness was making me sick. I felt like I had to throw up again, but I was able to suppress it.

"Hi, is he ready for me?" I asked, cutting any future conversations she was ready to start.

"Yes, he is. He's been waiting on you for a week, dear," she said, smiling so big that her cheeks began to turn red.

"Thanks."

I walked to his office and walked straight into the room like before.

"Hello Venus, or is it Mars?" he asked, catching me off guard and causing me to stop in my tracks.

"It's Venus," I corrected him with an attitude, sitting down in the chair.

"Ok, just making sure, you know. You never know with that conniving alter ego of yours," he said, taking a seat in his chair. *The fuck he means conniving alter?* I was two seconds from spazzing on the fuck, but I was able to keep calm.

"Dr. Burke, what makes you think Mars couldn't survive out in this world without Venus, but Venus can survive without Mars?" I asked, almost giving myself away.

"Well, Mars isn't real, so without Venus, there is no Mars. Mars is just a figment of your imagination, like an imaginary friend. She can go away, but you have to make her. You have to deal with whatever it is that keeps you holding on to her like you need her. You need to find comfort and security in someone else. Someone that you can trust, someone who brings positivity in your life instead of negativity. Someone like Ladonis. How is Ladonis anyway?" he asked. I shrugged my shoulders indicating that I didn't know.

"You don't know? Aren't you still staying with him at 2432 River Drive Hoboken, New Jersey?"

"Yea, I mean, we had a little fight and we're not really on speaking terms, so I'm not sure how he's doing," I said, cleaning up my lie. He sat there staring at me oddly.

"Venus, when you didn't show up last week for your session, I went to pay you a visit at Ladonis's condo which is located at 1600

Harbor Boulevard in Weehawken, New Jersey. When I asked the door man for Mr. Dawson's apartment number, he informed me that Mr. Dawson had been in the hospital for close to three months because he was struck by a vehicle. He also said that you were with him when it happened and that you drove off with another gentleman and he hadn't seen you in weeks. Where have you been staying, Venus? I can't possibly see how you managed to stay sane after witnessing Ladonis's near death experience when in fact, your session the day before the incident, you told me you loved him. I can't even imagine how devastated you were. That kind of devastation can drive anybody to a breaking point." I sat there trying to come up with a lie, but I had nothing.

"Yea, well I'm different. I'm stronger than before. so much so I don't even need these useless sessions with you. I'm out," I said, getting up from the chair and headed towards the door.

"Oh, and uh, Mars, if you're going to try and play Venus, you should learn the address."

"What?" I asked.

"Yea, I asked you the address two different times and two different addresses, and you agreed to both when in fact Ladonis's address is 1600 Harbor Boulevard in Weehawken, not Hoboken, not Jersey City. I'll be passing along my notes to Director Porter," he said, looking at me then back down to the papers in front of him. I walked out of the office, shutting the door behind me.

When I got to the car, Trub immediately knew something was wrong.

"What happened, Mars?" he asked.

"He knows," I answered.

"How the fuck did that happen?"

"I got Lodi's address wrong. He caught me in a lie," I said, picking up my purse and digging through it for Venus's wallet. When I found it, I opened it and pulled out her ID and looked at the address.

"Shit!" I said out loud. The address clearly read 1600 Harbor Blvd. If only my ass had looked through her shit, I probably wouldn't be on the verge of going back to the nut house. I looked through the wallet more and found a few hundred dollars and a few of Ladonis's credit cards.

"So what you trying to do?" Trub asked.

"What you think? That nigga's life has just hit its expiration. I can't go back to that place."

"What's your doctor's name?"

"Malcolm Burke, why?" I questioned. He never answered me, just took out his phone and dialed a number.

"Yo, Seth. I need a favor. Ya baby momma still works down at the DMV?" he asked.

"Yea, why?"

"I need you to call her and ask her to run a name for me and let me know the make and model of a car owned by Malcolm Burke. He's a psychologist for Edna Mahan Correctional Center.

"Aight, say no more my nigga," he said, hanging up the phone with Trub. Trub pulled to the back of the parking lot where we waited for Seth to call him back. We sat there for about 45 minutes when his phone started ringing.

"Is it him?" I asked anxiously. He shook his head up and down before answering his phone.

"Aight, cool," he said, hanging his phone back up.

"He said it's a hunter green jaguar with the license plate DOC MB1. How fucking obvious," he said, putting his car in drive and circled the parking lot until we came across the car. He pulled right next to it and we waited. I wasn't sure of the plan, but I knew this nigga had to die. I couldn't risk him going back to the director on me. Two hours later, he came strutting out the building like he was in a fashion show. I never noticed until now that he may be a little fruity.

It was just starting to get dark outside, so this was perfect timing. Trub and I had already switched seats, so I was now in the driver's seat and he was in the back seat. Dr. Burke was walking directly into our web. He clicked the remote to unlock his doors as he got closer to the car. Just as he was about to get into his car, Trub jumped out on him, placing him in a headlock. Dr. Burke tried to fight him off, but Trub outweighed him by at least 50 pounds. Dr. Burke was a frail little man who I probably could have taken down myself, but I wasn't going to take a chance. For all I knew, this man could have been ninja trained or some shit.

"Don't kill him," I said to Trub who still had Dr. Burke in the hold.

"I'm not," he responded, now dragging Dr. Burke back to the

car. Dr. Burke's body went limp as Trub threw him inside the car and shut the door and then jumped in the driver's side.

"Is he dead?"

"No, just sleeping. Let's get out of here. I'll send Mike back for the car."

We pulled out the dark parking lot and on to the road.

"So what you plan on doing with him?" he asked me.

"I don't know; kill him, I guess. Can't keep him alive, he might snitch on me."

"Not if I have the boys rough him up a little. We not killing him, Mars." I looked over at him.

"What happened to you being this big time scary nigga in the hood?"

"I am, for those niggas who cross me or disrespect me or stop my money. This dude ain't done any of the above. If yo' ass had taken this playing Venus shit serious, maybe you wouldn't be in this predicament. Did that ever cross your mind?" he questioned with his focus between the road and his cell phone.

"Stop complaining, grandpa. Just let me kill him and that'll be that. He really tried to play me out back in that office, calling me conniving and imaginary. I should let him feel how real I am by blowing his fucking brains out." He didn't respond, he just kept on driving and texting. I rolled my eyes and started staring outside, as the car continued to move down the highway. I felt myself getting sick again.

"What the fuck?" I said out loud.

"Pull the car over, I got throw up. Maybe it's motion sickness or something," I said, before I opened the door and threw up all over the side of the road.

****

Two hours later, we were inside the warehouse where Dr. Burke was getting the ass whipping of his life, as I sat front and center enjoying every moment of it.

Trub had all his boys meet us at the factory on the river. Even Lynea showed up with Peabo, Mike, LD and the nigga I was supposed to kill this week. I ain't forget about that shit. Little did he know, he was about to be my example. We were all gathered around in a circle as the boys took turns slamming their fists and knees into Dr. Burke's midsection.

"Dr. Burke, all you have to do is agree to keep ya mouth shut and make me believe it. You possibly telling the director or my program worker, I can get sent back to Edna where I definitely don't need to be. Do you know how many people will die if I go back there? Remember CO Barbra's little slip in the shower room? Yea, that wasn't no slip. In fact, that was a fall. A very, very hard fall that I may have caused. I didn't like the way the dike was staring at me while I was in the shower. Oh, and remember the girl Lexi who was mysteriously poisoned? Yep, it was me, mystery solved.

Every day I would dip her toothbrush in rat poison, but the bitch just wouldn't die. So late one night, I waited for the overnight staff to sneak off for his little quickie with Tasia, and I snuck out my room and into hers, and that's when I poured the rat poison down her throat and held the pillow over her face. Overkill, right? I know. I just really like the sight of death. You know I've been killing since I was nine years old. The first person I ever killed was the wife of the man that raped Venus. He really did a number on poor little Venus. That's where I came in.

See, after he raped her, he thought he was going to just walk away, no consequences, no nothing, but no. I had another plan for him. I snuck out of my bedroom and followed him home. The home where he shared with his wife and his daughter," I said, stopping and replaying the whole scene from almost 12 years ago back in my head. I was remembering it like it was yesterday… the feel of the knife going inside the wife's stomach and the smell of the fire and the look of the little girl who I left to die. That's when it hit me. I was looking this bitch in the face this whole time. I looked at Lynea and smiled. I wonder if she knew who I was. I knew I wasn't tripping. I knew them eyes from somewhere. It was her, the little girl from that night. I guess I was about to find out as I continued my story.

"I tricked his wife into allowing me into the house. When she did, I stabbed the bitch over and over and over again, and left her lying on her living room floor bleeding." I looked up at Lynea who was staring at me with cloudy eyes. I could see the tears forming in her eyes; that was the confirmation that I needed. She was indeed the little girl from that night.

"Now, the husband on the other hand, I made him suffer. That same little dick he raped Venus with, I cut it smooth off and then electrocuted his ass. That's when the house caught on fire and I knew I had to get my ass out that house, but first I stopped and thought I would give that little girl in the other room a friendly warning that she was about to die. But her little dumb ass just sat there staring at me like she was stuck on fucking stupid. I left her ass right there to burn with her parents. I wonder if she made it out," I said, standing up from my chair and now smiling at Lynea, who had managed to let the tears that were caught up in her eyes to fall. I looked around the room and everyone seemed a little confused as to what was going on.

"You fucking liar! My father wouldn't do no shit like that!" she burst out.

"Yea he did, that's why he's dead now. You know, at one point I thought he was doing it to you and I kind of felt bad for you, but now I don't. I should have barricaded yo' ass in that room and let you burn down with the house. I have a question. How did you know it was me? I can tell you knew just by the way you looked at me with anger and disgust. You hate me, don't you?" I asked her with a smile on my face. I was really enjoying this. I knew it was a reason why I was getting bad vibes from this chick.

"That day I seen you beat that crackhead mother of yours down in the hallway, I looked in your eyes and knew. Those horrid eyes of yours has haunted me for years and when I saw you in the hallway that day, I knew it was you. There can't be two people with those eyes in the world. Ya mother was right, she should have killed yo' ass when she found out she was pregnant with you."

"And ya father should have stayed at home and raped you instead of another man's child," I added. I guess that was the icing on the cake because she charged at me, knocking me to the floor. We started tussling and pulling at each other's hair. She was on top of me as she grabbed a fist full of my hair and started slamming my head against the floor. I felt myself starting to become dizzy. I reached for the wood plank that came from the chair that Dr. Burke was sitting in when we first brought him to the factory. It was broken when J-Mac kicked him out the chair. When I was able to reach it, I gripped it and brought it up against her head. Her head started to leak and she fell on to her back, as I climbed on top of her and was about to beat this bitch to death with this piece of wood. I felt myself being lifted off of her and then saw Peabo lifting Lynea up off the ground. Even with her head leaking and blood in her eyes, she still tried to come after me, but Peabo had a good grip on her. I tried to go after her, but Trub had a banging ass grip on me. Peabo walked Lynea out the door and seconds later, I heard them drive off. Trub still had me by my waist.

"I'm good, let me go," I said, snatching away from him. I spit out a mouthful of blood. That bitch Lynea really had some hands on her.

"Aye you," I called getting everyone's attention and they all looked at me.

"Didn't I promise to kill you this week because you had shit to do last week?"

"Bitch, you better go on about ya business," his disrespectful ass said. I pulled Trub's gun out and shot him twice in the face.

"I always keep my word, Dr. Burke, so I suggest you get far away from Jersey because if I end up back in Edna, I promise you, I'll come for you and I'll find you, and I will make you suffer the worst death ever," I said, walking out the factory doors.

LODI

Two Months Later

"Great job, Ladonis. You know, I've never seen anyone get as far as you have come in this short amount of time."

"I have shit to handle, Ms. Joann," I said, continuing to balance myself on the parallel bars and complete my 15-step goal that Joann set for me today. I had been working hard day and night to get my ass out this wheelchair. Even when Joann would leave, I would still be in the gym or home, working myself out. I was determined to be up and walking in two months, so I had no time to bullshit.

"Three more steps and then you can rest."

"Nah, let's keep going," I said, taking my final step.

"No, Ladonis. Pushing yourself can do more damage than good. You need to rest yourself," Joann said, but I ignored her and continued to walk past the point of expectation. My knees were a little sore but I wasn't giving in.

"You know what, Ladonis? If you won't listen to me then you don't need my services anymore."

"Yes, I do, Joann. You just need to understand that I'm not one of your pussy ass clients you may have attended to in the past. I know what my body can handle; I need you to trust me when I say to push me. At the end of the day, I'm paying you whether I walk or whether I fall. Now get over here and make this money, woman, or do I need to find another physical therapist?" I asked her.

"Ok, but tomorrow I will have you sign a waiver giving me permission to use excessive therapy treatment. I don't need to be sued or lose my license all because of ya bone head ass," she said, coming over and assisting me to my chair.

"Yo bro, you ready?" Jay asked, walking into the treatment room.

"Nah, not yet. Give me another hour," I said to her.

"Alright. Well, while you rest, check these out," Jay said, handing me a folder. I opened it and pulled out the pictures. Looking down on them and putting two and two together from the images, my heart damn near broke in two. I couldn't believe my eyes.

"What you wanna do, bro?"

"What you mean what I wanna do? I'm still bringing her home. This shit don't mean anything to me," I said, handing the pictures back to Jay. I rolled my chair over to the leg press and shifted myself over to the bench.

"Jay, you can come back in an hour and Ms. Joann, you can leave too. I'll see you tomorrow," I said putting my earphones on and turning up my DJ Khaled album. I was bothered by what I seen in those pictures and I was beyond pissed off that I didn't want to be bothered by anyone.

Later that night after I had Jay drop me off at home, I showered and then went and sat out on my balcony. I managed to grab the pictures out of Jay's car. I pulled them out the folder and looked at them again. I glided my hand across her beautiful face and then down and across her protruding belly. It wasn't too big, it just looks like she ate a big ass Thanksgiving meal, but seeing that and the women's health clinic building they were coming from, I knew in fact that Venus was pregnant. I looked out for her for five years while she was in Edna and for some reason, this didn't seem any different. I loved Venus and I was willing to accept the responsibility of taking care of her and her baby. I just wished it was my baby she was carrying. I sparked up a blunt and sat outside smoking before I went to bed.

The next morning, I woke up and my mother had come over and cooked me breakfast. At the same time, Joann had arrived for my morning physical therapy session. Me, her, and my mother sat there talking for a little while, before my mother had to leave and do whatever it is that she spent her time doing.

"Ms. Joann, let me get your opinion on something," I said to her, as I rolled my chair over to the table and got the folder. When I got back to the table, I took the pictures out and set them on the table.

"Now, I know she's pregnant, there's no denying that, but in your opinion, how far along do you think she is?" I asked her.

"Well, from my previous experience of being a midwife, I would say she could be about four months, could be going on five, maybe," she said. I picked up the pictures and started looking at them again for the millionth time. Last night, I thought I was going to be able to smoke and go to sleep, but I couldn't get the pictures out of my head. I kept thinking of the possibilities of that baby being mine. I started doing some research and they say a woman doesn't start showing until around four or five months, and they even had a size chart up. I compared the size chart to the picture of Venus and that also calculated that she could be about four or five months. If this is true, it was a possibility that that baby may be mine.

"Do you know this girl?" Joann asked.

"Yes, I do, but I don't want to talk about how I know her. Let's just get to work so I can get strong enough to bring her back home where she belongs."

TRUB

"Ok, here's your next target," Ma Dukes said, handing us some picture of a nigga dressed in a red fur coat.

"Who the fuck is this nigga looking like Gossamer from Looney Tunes?" Peabo asked.

"That is a man by the name of Cali. He's the new reign supreme nigga up west. He's known for being a grimy, snake nigga who probably has a bounty on his head by every nigga in the United States. But no one has been able to catch the nigga slipping. For one, he's smaller than a fucking midget and he has big ass bodyguards who tower him when walking, so no one has been able to get a shot off the nigga. You two need to be that one in a million who does knock him off his throne. He has money out the ass and drugs to supply the entire earth," Ma Dukes said. I continued to look over the picture and couldn't see what the fuck was the big deal with catching this nigga. He didn't look like a smart individual. He was too flashy, he stood out clear with a I'm either a pimp or a drug dealer target on his back. When I was done looking over the picture, I threw it on the coffee table and sat back on the couch.

"How you feeling, baby luv?"

"Fine. Can I come with y'all to do this?" Mars asked.

"You must've bump ya fucking head," I said, reaching over and trying to rub her baby bump, but she smacked my hand away. I don't know what it was with her not allowing me to touch her

101

stomach. I had to manhandle her ass just to get a feel of my baby.

I reached over again and attempted to rub her belly, but once again, she tried to smack my hand away. I grabbed both of her hands and locked them in one of my big hands, and rubbed her belly. She tried to fight me but couldn't really do much without hands.

When I was satisfied with my feels, I let her hands go and she used her feet and tried to kick me, but I caught her feet and held them until she stopped kicking. When she finally did, I caressed her feet like I did for her every night. Mars was mean in general, but with this pregnancy, she was meaner and hormonal. I couldn't wait to meet my baby. I was excited to be a father, and Ma Dukes and Peabo were excited as well. The only one who wasn't excited for us was Lynea. Her and Mars were still at odds, but the fighting seized once we found out Mars was pregnant. I told Lynea if she put her hands on Mars while she was pregnant with my kid, I would body her ass my damn self.

"Aww, look at you two. I can't wait to meet her," Ma Dukes said.

"Her? This here is my little prince."

"No, I have a sixth sense for these things. I will bet my life that this baby is a girl."

"Enough about the fetus, why can't I come, y'all? I can stay in the car," Mars said.

"Then what use are you? Just stay ya fat ass home," Lynea said, rolling her eyes.

"Bitch, who the fuck you calling fat? I will kill yo' ass in this bitch," Mars said, getting up off the couch at the same time Lynea popped up off the couch too. I pulled Mars back down on the couch and Peabo did the same. I couldn't wait until Mars had this damn baby so these two could fight all they want.

"You know what, since I can't go, I'm out of here," Mars said, slipping on her sneakers and grabbing the car keys off the table. She stormed out the door with an attitude, making sure she slammed the door behind her.

Mars had gotten her license so she was able to drive as much as she wanted, wherever she wanted. I had brought her a little 2010 Honda Accord so that she would have something to get around in. She wanted a 2015 BMW X5, but I wasn't about to get her that shit just so she could crash.

"You need to check yo' girl before I smack her pregnant ass," Lynea said, pointing her finger at me.

"And you need to sit yo' ass down somewhere before I smack yo' ass," I replied, never looking up from the blunt I was putting together. I heard her suck her teeth but she knew not to challenge my word. She may have been my brother's girl, but I would still smack fire out of her or any bitch that had something smart to say, except Mars. I ain't gone lie, I was secretly a little scared of her ass. I've seen some of the shit she did. I wasn't trying to wake up missing a fucking ear or some shit because I done said something wrong to her little sexy, psycho ass. I finished rolling up the blunt and was admiring my work, when there was a knock on the door.

Peabo jumped up and ran to answer it.

"Yo, Ma Dukes, somebody at the door for you," Peabo yelled, walking back into the living room.

"No shit, it's my house," she responded, getting up from her stool.

I lit the blunt and took a few pulls from it before I handed it to Peabo, who took a few pulls and then passed it to Lynea. Ma Dukes came walking back into the living room followed by another woman. I didn't even bother to look up. I just took a glance and then looked at the TV as I started flipping through the channels.

"Hey boys and Lynea, this here is my friend, Nancy," Ma Dukes said. Hearing the name caused me to look up and this time focus on the woman standing before me. I hadn't seen her face in almost 15 years. She looked exactly the same, just a little older. I don't know how I was unable to recognize her when I first looked up. It was probably the weed in the way.

She stood there looking down at me with the most angelic smile I had ever seen. She was still as beautiful as ever.

"Hey son, you remember me?" she asked.

"Of course I remember you, Ma. I can never forget your face," I said, walking closer to her and pulling her in for a hug that felt like it lasted forever. Even when I felt her grip on me loosen up a little, mine still remained. When I was done, I let her go and just looked at her and she did the same to me. I didn't need to ask when she had got out because I could tell by her appearance it had to be recently. She had on some grey sweats, a sweatshirt, and a pair of beat down slide-ons that looked like they were straight from prison.

"Ma Dukes, why my moms look like this? I thought you were keeping her and my dad stacked?" I asked her.

"I tried, ole stubborn ass there wouldn't take it, but ya father did. I was putting $400 a month in their accounts, but because she wasn't using hers and it was stacking up, they stopped me from depositing and sent me a check for almost two grand back. Miss Thing here wouldn't even allow me to come see her either, so I had no idea when she was getting out. I could have had a place already decked out for you, girl."

"I needed to learn to be free from the money. That's why your father and I are in the predicament we're in, because of money. We were some money hungry niggas back in the day, and nothing or no one was going to stop us from getting it, so we thought. Them pigs sure did prove us wrong, though. They got us for everything; money, house, car, clothes, they even tried to get my baby boy too, but you wasn't having that shit, ain't that right, baby?"

"Damn right, Ma. But look, I can't have you walking around like this. Let Ma Dukes take you shopping. I would take you but I have shit to handle."

"Maybe... she and I do have a lot to catch up on. I guess we can do that at the mall," my mother said.

"Cool, and make sure you're here when I get back. As a matter of fact, here, take my key. Ma Dukes, drop her off at my place.

Mars should be there anyway, you two need to meet."

"Ooo, who's Mars, your girlfriend?" my mother asked, poking me in the stomach like a school girl.

"His baby momma," Lynea said, rolling her eyes.

"You have a baby on the way? I'm going to be a grandma?"

"Alright, now listen here, woman. Don't be coming up in here trying to take my grandbaby from me, aight?" Ma Dukes interfered.

"Hold up, he came out my thang, but you helped raise him, so it's as much your grandbaby as it will be mine. I can't wait to be a Na Na," my mother, said jumping up and down.

"Alright, calm ya horses. I'll see you later. Let's be out, y'all," I said to Peabo and Lynea. When we got on the hallway, I slapped Lynea right upside the back of her head. I was tired of her attitude towards Mars and I know if I had slapped her in front of Ma Dukes, she would have pounced on my ass for hitting a female.

"Nigga, what the fuck you do that for?" Peabo asked.

"Because I'm sick of her attitude and shit. Get the fuck over it. You can't be mad at her for protecting herself from a rapist. Get over it, Lynea."

"That heffa is a crazy, murderous lunatic, and that baby she's pregnant with is going to be exactly the same," she said storming off. I had never thought about it that way. I know there is something wrong with her mentally and I wasn't sure how the baby was going to be affected by it. What if this other personality, Venus, came back, and tried to run back to that nigga Lodi? Fuck that, she could go, but my baby is staying.

I followed them outside, and we all hopped in Peabo's truck with the rest of the crew following behind in another truck. On the way to this dude Cali's crib, I was lost in my thoughts. My mind was full of the 'what ifs'. I pulled my phone out and texted Mars to see if she had made it home. I sent her a message and set my phone on my lap, as I continued to think of the future. I heard a beep coming from the trunk area of the truck. The beep was familiar, a little too familiar. I turned around towards the back and I picked up my phone off my lap. I texted Mars's phone again and waited, and just like last time, the beep went off. I saw something move in the back.

"Hold the fuck up," I said, sitting up on my knees.

"What happened?" Peabo asked. I leaned over the back of the seat and looked in the trunk part of the car. I moved the blankets and shit that was back there, and immediately became mad but I couldn't help myself from laughing.

"What the hell yo' ass doing back here?" I said to Mars, who was in the back, balled up, trying to hide.

"I told you I wanted to come and you wouldn't let me, so I snuck in the back."

"How the hell you get in my car, girl?" Peabo asked as he continued to drive.

"You out of all people should know what happens in the hood when you don't lock your doors. Didn't Ma Dukes find you sleeping in an unlocked car?" Mars asked. Peabo just sat there quietly.

"Didn't I tell you to take yo' ass home?"

"Who the fuck do you think you are? You ain't my daddy. I didn't want to go to that house by myself. I'm here, so now what?" she said, climbing from the trunk space to the back seat.

"The fuck you mean now what? P, bust a motherfucking U-turn, we taking her ass home."

"Peabo, you turn this truck around, I'm busting you dead in the back of yo' head," Mars said.

"And if you touch my man, I'm busting you dead in yo' motherfucking eye, bitch," Lynea said.

"Shut the fuck up, both of y'all, before I put both of y'all on the side of the road. P, turn this bitch around now," I said becoming visibly upset. I had mad love for Mars, but I was really becoming fed up with her ass undermining me and thinking she could do what the fuck she wanted.

Peabo made a U-turn on the way, we stopped and told the other guys to go there and we'd meet them, and not to do anything until we got there.

The drive back to my house was quiet. Mars sat all the way across on the other side of the car, with her arms folded like she had an attitude. I ain't give a fuck. I wasn't about to let her put herself or my baby at risk.

"Fix ya face and lose the attitude, Mars. I'm only doing this because I love you and I don't want anything to happen to you or our baby," I said to her as we pulled up to my apartment building.

She ignored me and hopped out the car and slammed the door hard. The whole damn car shook.

"The fuck," Peabo said because of the way Mars slammed his door.

"She'll be aight, bro, let's just go," I said, as I watched her walk in the front door of the building.

We pulled off down the street and on to the road.

"You know what, P, just drop me off at my place, I'm not in the mood for this shit anymore. That bitch just ruined a good time," Lynea said.

"We need you, Nea."

"Y'all don't need my ass. I'm sure y'all had a plan B if shit went south. Use that," she said. I don't know what the fuck was wrong with the women today, but I wasn't beat for this shit.

"P, just drop her ass off so we can get going." He turned off the road and a few minutes later, we were pulling up in front of Lynea's house. She jumped out and went straight in the house, and we hopped on the road and was on our way to handle business.

MARS

I walked in the house heated, and on top of that, hormonal. I was pissed the fuck off at Trub. I don't know who the fuck he thought he was, trying to tell me what the fuck to do. I had something for his ass.

I walked in our bedroom and into the closet, and took out all his Retro Jordans and brought them to the kitchen. I went to the refrigerator and took out the ketchup, mustard and relish. I got a knife and started cutting up every pair of his Jordans. He had every single pair that ever came out, so it took me a while to get them all. When I did, I put them all inside the bathtub and went back to the kitchen and got the condiments. I took the ketchup and mustard, tipped them over, and started squirting them all over the cut up Jordans until they were covered, and then did the same thing with the relish. When I was done, I stood there looking at them. I wasn't quite satisfied just yet. I went to the drawer of the vanity and found the matches. I lit one up and threw it in the tub on the mess. I sat there and watched it burn for a few, or at least until I was satisfied, and then I turned on the shower and let the water run over it, putting out the flames.

"Trub is going to kill yo' ass," I heard someone say behind me. I turned around to this bitch standing there looking like she was ready for war.

"What the fuck yo' ass doing in here?" I asked her.

"Bitch, I have a key."

"Ok, but that doesn't explain why you are here now. I thought you went tagging along with them?"

"Nope, I didn't. I made them drop me off. This was my only opportunity to get you alone with no interruptions."

"Smart little hoe... I grew a little respect for yo' ass for plotting this one."

"Yep," she said before she came running full speed towards me, knocking me into the sink. My back hit the sink so hard there was no way I should have been able to still walk. I grabbed on to her face and dug my nails into her skin. My plan was to pull her damn cheekbone through her face. She started screaming like a damn banshee while trying to raise her foot to kick me in the stomach. I spun around and slammed her back into the vanity mirror and the glass shattered. With my fingers still dug into her face, I kneed her in the pussy hard. I could hear her breath get caught in her throat as she fell to the floor.

"You wanna play with me, bitch," I screamed out loud like a mad woman.

"I got something for that ass."

I stomped her in the face before I went to the medicine cabinet and took out my nail polish remover, opened it and dumped it all over her. She tried to get up but I kicked the hoe dead in her face. I got the matches that I already had out when I set the Jordans on fire, and struck one.

"Say what up to your pops for me," I said before I threw the lit match on top of her. Her body slowly started going up in flames thanks to the nail polish remover. She started rolling all over the floor, yelling and screaming trying to put out the fire, but she was only making it worst because it was nail polish on the floor as well. I stood there watching as the flames danced around her body, torturing her. She stood up and ran in to the hallway towards the bedroom. I followed her out into the hallway and continued to watch her, when I felt someone grab me from behind. I couldn't see their face because whoever this was had on a mask. The other intruder ran over to Lynea and threw a blanket over her, putting out the flames.

I wasn't sure who these people were but I tried to fight my way out of their grasp. The other person who had just helped Lynea ran over to me and took something out of their pocket. I was able to clearly see that it was a brown bottle and a rag. I knew immediately that it was chloroform.

"Stop, no, I'm pregnant," I yelled hoping that this would work in my favor. Me saying I was pregnant caused the person to actually stop what they were doing.

"Just use a little bit on her ass. A little shouldn't harm the baby," the one holding me said.

"Maybe we should call Lodi," the other one asked.

"No, just do it. If you call him, for one, he's going to be pissed we're even doing this and two, he's going to say not to use the chloroform. I can already tell you if we take her up out of here using this chloroform, she's going to put up a fight. Trust me, a little won't harm the baby."

The other person continued with their task and then placed the rag over my mouth. I tried moving my face but that wasn't going to help; the room was already starting to spin and that was the last thing I remembered before it all went black.

****

I woke up to a dark room. I couldn't see where I was because all the lights were out and it was nothing but the street lights from outside shining through the window. I sat up in the bed and instantly caught a headache. I got off the bed and went looking for the light switch. I felt against the wall until I found it, and flipped it on. I looked around the cozy little bedroom and didn't recognize where I was. I looked out the window and looked up and down the unfamiliar block. I had no idea where I was, but I damn sure was about to find out. I lifted the window and a loud noise rang out.

"Fuck," I said, as I moved the chair that was next to the bed against the window. I climbed in the chair and then up into the window pane. Some dude with braids came running inside the room.

"Oh shit," he said, running into the bedroom just as I gained the balls to take the leap out the window. *Tuck and roll, tuck and roll* was what I kept thinking as I jumped with preparation to hit the ground, but that didn't go the way I had planned. The braided head fuck was as able to catch me just in time before I jumped. He dragged me back in the window and into the room, and threw me on the bed. I jumped back up, picking up the lamp that was on the side dresser and throwing it at his head. He ducked it and came walking over towards me. I picked up the FIOS remote and threw that at him, tagging him dead in the nose. He wasn't expecting my good as reflexes to pick up that remote so fast.

"Fuck!" he yelled out in pain and held on to his nose. I took the opportunity and jumped on to the bed and over to the other side of the room, and then darted out the bedroom door. I ran down the hall and then down the stairs. The front door was right there and I was headed straight to that motherfucker Usain Bolt style, pregnant belly and all. I was halfway down the stairs when Lodi came rolling his cripple ass in from another room, catching me off guard, but not too off guard because I was still heading for the door. *What the hell was cripple going to do, run my feet over?* I thought, just as I jumped off the last step. Lodi stood up from his wheelchair and grabbed me. I started fighting my way out of his grasp, but he had a good grip on me. I couldn't go anywhere if I tried.

"Calm down before you hurt the baby," he said.

"Why the fuck do you care about this baby? Now let me go," I demanded, fighting even harder.

"I care because this baby is inside my girl, and whether I'm the father or not, I'm still going to care for her and that baby like it's mine," he said.

"Yea, well it's not so can that thought, Romeo, and let me the hell up out of the house."

"Tell me this one thing. How far along are you?"

"I'm seventeen weeks, why?" I answered. He sat there quietly and tried to hide the smile that appeared on his face and then disappeared.

"The hell you smiling for?"

"Seventeen weeks will put you around the same time your little boyfriend hit me with his car."

"Ok, and you're telling me this because?" I asked him sarcastically.

"Because five hours before that, Venus and I made love every hour on the hour. The same thing happened the day before that and the day before that. It's a strong possibility that that baby can be mine just as much as it could be your little stick up boy's, but he's not going to live long enough to be a father, so you can kill that dream right here."

"If you touch him I swear to God I'll throw myself off a building and there will be no more Venus and no more baby, partner."

"I'm just not understanding why yo' ass won't just go away," he said. I looked up at him and laughed.

"Man, shut up, over there sounding like a little bitch. I don't understand why you just won't go away," I mimicked what he had just said but in a whining little girl voice.

I gave up fighting him and sat down on the steps. I was starting to have stomach cramps. I think all the fighting and aggressive movements were bothering this kid.

"It's not me that won't go away; I can't just go away because at the end of the day I'm not real, so everyone keeps saying. Venus is the controller here. Obviously, she don't want me to go away.

She thought you were dead and so did I, and that left her with no one. Her black ass friend has been spending her time getting her pussy licked by ya butch ass sister, and her mother is a crackhead who killed her when she was nine and end up brining her back to life by mistake. That's her issue, she thinks she has no one. And Venus can't survive in a world with no one, she's not about that life. I'm all she has, buddy boy.

"Hold up, go back. Did you say she died when she was nine?"

"You deaf, nigga? Yes, the same night her mother sold her to be raped, Venus's crack whore mother strangled her to death, trying to get rid of me; plan failed. She was in one of her crackhead rages and instead of her just strangling her and keeping it pushing, she tried to be greedy and overkill it by stomping Venus, which actually did more good than bad. She restarted Venus's heart. When Venus woke up, Jessica called her all kind of Satan's and the devil's spawn, and poor little Venus had no idea what was going on.

I would always remind her of that night just so I could get loose and kill that mother of hers. I really wanted to make her suffer but for some reason, Venus continues to hold onto the good her mother once had. Venus never deserved the hell she was put through. Even in her foster home, her foster mother mistreated her. She had it rough. I think her way of temporary suicide is me. I numb her to the pain of her miserable life. What you think is going to happen when she comes to and sees this belly? You think she's going to be happy and start thinking wedding bells, and house and dogs and white picket fences and shit? Nope. She's going to think rape, murder, beatings, death, and me, her scapegoat. She's a lost cause, Ladonis. Give her up because until she starts seeing better things in life, there is always going to be a Mars in the picture, boo."

"Nah, not after I show her this," he said, pulling out a black box and opening it, revealing a beautiful diamond ring. I had to admit, even I was a little jealous of the damn ring, but I had to play it cool. I started laughing obnoxiously as I stood up.

"Ok, lover boy. Look, I have somewhere to be so are you going to let me out this house, or am I going to have to beat yo' big ass down to get up out this bitch?"

"Option two, because I ain't letting you leave," he said, sitting back down in his wheel chair.

"And what you finna do, run me over with ya wheelchair?" I asked.

"If I have to."

"Fine," I said running towards the back of the house. There had to be a back door somewhere. I looked behind me and he was really chasing me in his wheelchair. This shit was comical; I couldn't even continue to run because I was laughing so hard. My laughing soon turned to cries of pain as the cramping in my stomach started to get worse by the seconds.

"What's wrong with you?" Ladonis asked.

"The baby."

"Shit, come on," he said picking me off the floor and on to his lap, as he rolled back towards the living room.

"Loc, we gotta go," he yelled upstairs, and the dude I bust in the head with the remote controller came down the stairs.

"What happened?" he asked, walking down the stairs with tissue hanging out his nostrils that was being used to stop the bleeding.

"I don't know, but I need you to take her to the hospital quick. I'll be right behind y'all." The other guy came and got me and started walking me out the door to the car.

"I should drop yo' ass right on ya damn head, busting my nose and shit."

"Shut the fuck up and get me to that damn hospital before I rip yo' damn tongue out. We got to the car and he laid me in the back seat, and then he went around and got in the driver's seat and pulled off.

I wasn't sure what was going on, but I was in so much pain, and I've hardly ever felt pain until this moment. This was an unbearable pain that not even I could handle. Fuck this shit, Venus was on her own. There was nothing left for me anymore. Ladonis wasn't letting me leave. After seeing that ring, I knew right then that Venus was going to be okay. I just wish that I had the chance to say bye to Trub. It pains me to know that the last thing he'll remember me by is cutting and burning his Jordans.

VENUS

"Ahhh," I cried out in pain as I laid balled up in the back seat of a car. I felt like I had been dead and brought back to life just to feel like I wanted to die. This pain I was in was by far the worst, but then again, all too familiar. I cupped my swollen belly as I continued to cry out in pain.

"Get the fuck out the way," I heard someone yell and recognized the voice of Loc. I rolled myself over in the back seat and saw Loc in the driver's seat.

"Loc," I called to him but he didn't answer.

"Loc," I called again this time louder.

"The fuck yo' crazy ass want?" Loc asked, never giving me eye contact, keeping his eyes on the road.

"Where's Lodi?" I asked him.

"Why the fuck you care? Just lay yo' ass back there and be quiet. The hospital is around the corner," he said. I did what he said because I figured he must've thought that I was still Mars; besides, talking was making the pain worse anyway. I continued to rock back and forth while balled up and cupping my stomach. Last thing I remember was Lodi getting hit by a car and me not having this stomach. *How long was I gone?* It had to have been a while because my belly was big. *Could I have been having another miscarriage?* Lord, I really hope I wasn't.

I was lost in my thoughts trying to forget about the pain I was in, when the car came to a quick stop. I slid off the back seat, hitting my face on the back of the passenger seat, and landing on the floor. The door came open and Loc took me out the car and carried me in his arms into the hospital. I looked up at him.

"Loc, where is Lodi?" I asked again because the last time I saw him, he was lying in the middle of the street on the verge of dying.

"Yo, stop asking about my boy," Loc said, running into the hospital.

"I need help. She's pregnant and having stomach pains," he said to the lady sitting at the front desk.

"Can we get a gurney," she called to the back. Seconds later, Loc was laying me onto the bed.

"Loc, it's me, Venus," I said before they pushed me away to the back.

LODI

I walked into the hospital's waiting room with my cane, looking for Loc. I would have brought my chair but I couldn't get that shit in the car. I told Loc to go ahead without me because my slow cripple ass would have taken forever to get in and out of the car. I did, however, drive myself here, which was a big improvement in my recovery, although I know once I told Joann she was going to be pissed the fuck off.

I found Loc over in the corner, scrolling through his phone.

"Yo," I called to him as I slowly walked over to him.

"What they saying?" I asked him.

"I don't know, they ain't come out yet but yo, I think it's actually Venus back there, not the other one. In the car, she kept asking about you but I ignored her ass and told her to shut up. When we got to the hospital, she asked for you again and when I laid her down on the bed, she said 'Loc, it's me, Venus,' and they pushed her ass in the back and told me to wait out here."

"Shit man, I hope she's not losing that baby," I said as I sat down next to him. As soon as I sat down, I immediately started feeling pain in my hips. I wasn't sure if I was going to be able to move my ass out this chair. I pulled out my phone and called Joann to tell her about the pain and if I should see a doctor while I was here. She told me it was normal, that it was just because I sat down and released the pressure of standing which caused the pain to come about. She called me hardheaded and told me to get off her phone, then she hung up on me.

"Family of Venus Morgan?" the doctor came out and asked. I jumped up, disregarding the pain that I had in my hips.

"That's me."

"And you are?" he asked.

"Her fiancé," I answered.

"Ok, she's doing good and so is the baby."

"Doc, why was she in so much pain?"

"I honestly can't tell you, but something was rattling the little guy up in that stomach. Did Ms. Morgan take a fall of some sort or maybe made some erratic movements?" he asked.

"Not that I know of, Doc, but did you say little guy? It's a boy?"

"Yes, it is. Come on, let me take you to your family," he said, guiding Loc and I to the back. When we got to her room, she was sitting up signing papers with one of the nurses. I leaned against the door with my cane as I sat there watching her.

"Hey you," I said catching her attention. She turned and smiled at me.

"Hey," she smiled that beautiful smile that I had missed so much. Her smile faded and then she started crying.

"What's the matter?" I asked her as I walked my cripple ass over to her. I climbed in the bed with her, pulling her into my arms.

"How is it that I'm pregnant, Lodi? What happened? Whose baby is it? What if it's not yours, Lodi?" she cried.

"Don't think about all that, V, baby. Everything is going to be cool. Whether I'm the father or not, that's still going to be my baby because you're gonna always be my girl."

"Lodi, I thought you were dead. I remember that day like it was yesterday; well, technically it was yesterday for me. This had to be the longest that I've ever been out. How can I be a good mother if I'm unstable? What if that shit happens to you again and I black out and leave the baby alone, or Mars comes back and try to play mommy?"

I let her go on and rant I just sat there listening to her. Truth be told, I missed her. I missed her voice, I missed everything about this woman. I sat there thinking if maybe now was the right time to give her the ring. I thought about everything Mars was saying earlier about Venus feeling alone.

"Hey, open this," I said setting the box on her lap. She stopped crying long enough to make out what it was and then she gasped for air. She wiped her face and reached down and picked it up. She opened it and the waterworks started again.

"But why?" she asked through tears.

"Because I love you and being without you for those four months really made me realize that I don't ever want to go that long again without your presence. For five years, you pushed me and kept me motivated. You are one of my best friends and they say you should marry your best friend, so it's either you or Loc. And if I gotta marry that nigga then my black ass ain't never getting married. I love you, Venus, and I don't want you to ever feel like you are alone in this world. You have a family… we have a family growing inside of you. My somewhat dysfunctional family will be your somewhat dysfunctional family. Your problems will be our problems and we'll solve them shits together. I just need for you to say you'll be my best friend and my wife for life, and you'll never want for anything." She sat there for a minute looking at the ring.

"How much did you pay for this?"

"Girl, don't worry about all that, just answer the question," I said to her.

"Yes, I'll be your wife for life," she answered. I lifted her face and kissed her lips. She wrapped her arms around my waist and pulled me down to her.

"Ahh shit, baby."

"Oh my God! I'm sorry, baby."

"Knock, knock," Loc said, walking into the room.

"Hey, Loc," Venus greeted.

"Hey, V. Look, I'm sorry for cursing at you back there in the car. I thought you were… well, you know. But anyway, I wanted to give you this," he said handing her a blue teddy bear.

"Aww, thanks Loc, you didn't have to."

"It's cool. Did I miss something?" he said, head nodding towards the bed. Venus and I both looked down. I had completely forgotten to put the ring on her finger after she said yes.

"Oh yea," I said picking up the ring and placing it on her finger.

"Ah shit, my man about to take that step. I applaud you, man. Marrying a woman is one thing but you about to marry two women, both in one woman's body. Two for the price of one. I want to be like you when I grow up," Loc's dumb ass said.

"Shut yo' ass up."

"Nah, for real. Congratulations, though. I'm about to get up out of here. I have a physical therapy session in 10 minutes. You good though, bro?" Loc asked me.

"Yea, I'm good. Make sure you out of there at a decent time. She better not be late for my therapy session at nine, tomorrow."

"Got you, man," he said, walking out the room door and into the hallway.

TRUB

"Yo Deez, grab Nutz and let's get out this bitch. This was a waste of my fucking time. I could have been at home with my mother and my girl. How the fuck y'all let that little nigga get away? Starting Monday, I'm getting me a whole new crew. Y'all bitches suck for real. And how the fuck you get shot in the damn foot?" I asked Nutz as Deez helped him walk to the car. The hit was a bust. That nigga Cali was able to slither his way right out the side door. These niggas were in here playing around, causing Cali to get away with the product and the money, but half his crew was still in here dead on the floor. That nigga really was a snake though. He was pushing some of his crew members in the line of fire so that he could get away. He may have gotten away, but I was eventually going to find that ass one way or another, and I put that shit on my unborn seed.

"Come on, P, drop me off home. Mars probably at the house mad as hell, burning all my shit up. Maybe I should stop and get her some roses or something," I said to Peabo and he laughed.

"What you laughing for?"

"Nigga, Mars is not the roses kind of girl. She looks like the guns and torch weapons kind of girl. Stop and get her ass a Taser from somewhere. I bet she'll forgive you."

"Yea, maybe… after she uses that shit on me. I ain't about to buy her shit she can torture my ass with. I can see it now, I'm sleep and I wake up to an electric shock because she went through my phone. Probably shit on myself," I said, just as my phone started ringing. I didn't recognize the number with the New York area code.

"Hello," I answered.

"Mr. Trouble, sir, this is Luis, the doorman. We have a bit of a situation at your apartment."

"What kind of a situation?" I asked.

"You should get here quickly before the police show up. I already called them," he said.

"Yo, Peabo, step on it. My doorman just called and said it was a problem at my place.

"What did he say, what kind of problem?"

"Nah, he just said to get there quick before the police show up."

"What the fuck?" he said pushing on the gas.

"Shit, I hope Mars ain't did no shit to my mother. I never called and told her she was coming," I said, as I took the phone from my ear and tried calling Mars again, but it went straight to voicemail. I hung up and called Ma Dukes to see if she dropped my mother off at my place, but she said her and my mother was still at her house catching up, so that was a good thing.

"Yo, you heard from Lynea?" I asked Peabo.

"Nah."

"Shit, you ain't find it kind of strange that she all of a sudden wanted to drop out the hit? Since when has she ever left us hanging like that?"

"Shit, that's true," Peabo said, realizing that same thing.

"I bet you any amount of money she done made her way over to Mars. If she hurts Mars or that baby, I'm punching her dead in her shit. I promise you, man."

With Peabo driving over 80 miles an hour, we got to my apartment in less than 15 minutes. I jumped out the car before it even had a chance to stop, and I ran into the building. The cops and ambulance were already there. I saw Luis and ran over to him.

"What happened?" I asked. He pointed to someone lying on the gurney. I took a closer look at the person who appeared to be burned badly, and I was able to make out the face. It was Lynea.

"Lynea, what happened? Where is Mars?" She didn't answer me, she just looked at me.

"We got to go," one of the emergency technicians said as they started rolling Lynea out the building. At the same time, Peabo had come into the building.

"What the fuck?" I heard him say as he ran up to her.

"Luis, what happened?" I asked him.

"I don't know, I was just sitting here when she came downstairs all burned and then she collapsed on the floor. I ran over and turned her over and recognized her as your sister, so I called the cops and then you. I went upstairs to your apartment but there was no one there."

"My girl ain't up there?"

"No one, Mr. Trouble, sir." I left him and ran upstairs to my place. When I walked inside, it smelled like burned flesh mixed with burned paper or some shit. I walked through the house looking for Mars and she was nowhere to be found. I did find that my bathroom was trashed and inside the tub was a mess. When I realized what was in tub, I almost had a bitch fit real quick, but that wasn't important right now. I pulled out my phone and called Mars again, and I heard her phone ringing inside the bedroom. *Where the fuck is this girl?* I asked myself. I went back downstairs, running into Peabo as I was coming out the elevator.

"Yo, did she anything?" I asked him.

"All she said was two people took Mars," Peabo said.

"Yo Luis, was you here all night?"

"Yes, I got in at five this afternoon and haven't left my post, only to go check on your place."

"Do you have cameras to the back door?"

"Yes, come, let me show you. Please don't say anything to my supervisor; I can get in really big trouble."

"We're not nigga, just show us the damn video," I said, becoming agitated by the second. He rolled the tape back a few hours and on the video, two guys entered the back door, wearing black hoodies and an hour later, the same two guys left out the back door carrying an unconscious Mars.

"Guarantee you it's that fucking Lodi. This nigga and everyone he loves needs to die now," I said seething. I pulled out my phone and called Seth, letting him know his services were going to be needed. Peabo wanted to go to the hospital to sit with Lynea, but I told him to let Ma Dukes go check on her; him and I had business

132

to attend to.

An Hour Later

"I heard you like to run your mouth, so tell me where I can find this Lodi nigga," I said to the doorman of the nigga Lodi's building, as I hung him over the balcony of Lodi's apartment. I believe he was the same one who was running his mouth to Dr. Burke about me running down Lodi and Mars not being around.

"I don't know, he hasn't been here all day and neither has the girl. I swear," he cried.

"I know you know where I can find him. Every concierge has the emergency information of every tenant in the building. I need that address from you now," I said.

"Ok. Please just let me down so that I can get it for you," he begged. I let him down from the balcony. This nigga was terrified. I can tell by the piss that was now streaming down his leg.

"Mikey, go with this nigga," I said, pushing him along with the pissy doorman.

"Why the fuck I gotta go with him?" he asked. I turned around and looked at him.

"Excuse you, nigga, what the fuck did you just say? You gotta go because I'm telling you to go. You know what," I said pulling out my gun and shooting him in the center of his head, immediately laying him out.

"Now yo' ass don't have to go no fucking where but to hell. You know what, you don't have to go anywhere either," I stated to the frightened front desk man as I picked his ass up and threw him over the balcony.

"Now y'all niggas tear this shit up until you find me some information on how I can get my girl back."

They all scattered into different rooms of the apartment, emptying out drawers and cabinets, and flipping over beds. I walked through the house, watching them tear the house up. I got into one of the bedrooms and I knew it belonged to Mars or Venus. The scent inside the room alone told me that she was here at some point, and that nigga ain't just get thrown off the balcony for no reason. On the dresser was a picture of her and that nigga Lodi. I picked it up and studied the picture. I became disturbed and bothered just seeing the way he was touching her in the picture. Crazy thing was that it wasn't her in the picture. It was Mars's body and face, but those green eyes weren't hers. They were the eyes of Venus. I pulled out my picture of Mars and I from the night we were on the boat, and compared the two pictures.

In the picture with Lodi, Venus is visibly happy with that nigga. This was apparent by the smile she had on her face. In the picture with me, Mars is expressionless, cold, unattached. Could it be that she wasn't happy with me like Venus was with Lodi? Was all this for nothing? Was it true that Mars was not real and was all just a phase that Venus needed to get over? What about that baby? How did I know that baby was mine and not the nigga Lodi's? She was 17 weeks pregnant. When I think about it, Mars has only been with me for sixteen maybe seventeen weeks. Nah, fuck that, that was my baby. I felt that shit in my bones, and I wasn't going to stop until I found out.

I picked up the computer chair that was in the room and smashed it against the mirror. I trashed the flat screen that was in the room along with the computer. I went through the house smashing all the TVs. I was really in my feelings and it was no stopping me. I was on a warpath of destruction.

"I found something," Deez said, running into the living room with a book in his hand. I took it from him and opened it, and started flipping through the pages. It was an address book. It was a few names in there, I wasn't sure which one was who, but I was making a stop at every house in this book until I found my girl.

"Burn this shit," I said to them as I walked out the apartment.

LODI

"Yo Pops, what's up?" I asked, answering my cell phone.

"Son, have you seen the news?"

"Nah, why, what's up?"

"Turn on the news, there was a fire at your apartment building."

I reached over a sleeping Venus and grabbed the remote to turn on the TV. I turned to Channel 12 because I know that's the only news station my father watched. When I turned on the TV, there was my building, surrounded by smoke.

"What the fuck happened?" I watched more where they reported of the doorman Joe was found dead on the side of the building. It appeared he had been thrown to his death. It also reports that the point of origin of the fire came from apartment 6B and how they found someone dead inside the apartment, but they are not sure if it's the apartment's owner.

"What the fuck?" I shouted, which caused Venus to wake up. I sat there stunned, looking at the TV. That was my apartment where the fire started and where they were claiming Joe was thrown from. I already knew it was that motherfucking Trub nigga. He probably was looking for Mars.

"What's wrong, baby?" Venus asked, sitting up in the bed. I turned off the TV.

"Nothing, go back to sleep," I said, kissing her on the forehead and she laid back down. I got out the bed and walked out the room.

I pulled out my cell phone and called Loc. It took him about five rings before he answered the phone, sounding out of breath.

"Nigga, you good? You sound like you about to die," I joked.

"I'm good, what's up?" he asked.

"That nigga Trub just tried to burn my apartment building down and he killed Joe and someone else that was inside the apartment, but they couldn't tell who because the body was burned."

"The fuck. That nigga want ya girl back that bad?"

"Look, it's not about the girl no more, it's about the respect, and I heard this nigga will kill ya momma for that shit. I have a feeling he's coming after everyone; we gotta get them out of here."

"Nigga, it's not much you can do. That nigga is on the hunt and he ain't stopping until he gets you. We got to get to him first. I think you should take everyone somewhere away from here until shit dies down. Jay and I and some of the niggas will stick around and deal with this shit. You are not in the best condition to be trying to go to war with anyone."

"I'm fine. I'm going with y'all, it's a done deal. I can send everyone with my pops on a vacation somewhere. I don't need them getting involved with shit going on between myself and this dude," I stated. I don't know why the fuck he thought I would agree to running away from a fight. This fight was over my girl, so I needed to be there. It was me who he had a hit out on so I needed to finish this as soon as possible, if I wanted him out of Venus's life.

"You can barely walk my nigga."

"I'll be alright. Let me hit you back, I need to see when they going to allow Venus to leave," I said, hanging up the phone. I walked back in the room and Venus was sitting up in the bed.

"Mars started all this, didn't she? This is all my fault," Venus asked.

"She did, but there was nothing you could have done to prevent it. This dude is just a nigga in love. I would do the same thing if I was in his position. I would be on the hunt for you too, baby. Look, did they say how long you would have to stay in the hospital?"

"I just have to stay overnight."

"Cool, so they wouldn't be mad if I took you up out of here tonight." I went looking for a nurse. When the doctor was able to come talk to me, it took a lot of persuasion and promises, but I was able to get her released with the promise of having a midwife look after her for the next few weeks, and she had to stay on bedrest. Before we left the hospital, I called Joann and fired her as my physical therapist and hired her as Venus's midwife.

VENUS

Few Days Later...

Jamila and I sat in the living room watching the overly sexy older woman rub all over Lodi's muscles. I wasn't sure how I felt about that.

"So what part of the therapy is this?" I asked, referring to her hand on the inside of his thigh, a little too close to his privates.

"Oh stop, V, she doesn't want Lodi's black ass. She's married and if I heard right, she's fucking with Loc."

"What? That woman could be his mother."

"Girl, do she look like she could be somebody's mother? Hell no. Shit, if I was a man, I would try and hit her old ass too. She's one sexy senior citizen," Mila said.

"You are truly becoming fully gay, and here I was thinking it was a phase you were going through."

"Nope, Jay is my baby for life. Check out my tat," she said, lifting her shirt and revealing a big tattoo on her lower back that read JJ4L.

"What does that mean?"

"Jay and Jamila for life. We both got one." I looked at her like she was stupid.

"Were you not in the car when she admitted to being a whore?" I asked her.

"Yeah, but she wouldn't play me out. She knows I don't play with her ass. I'll fuck her butch ass up."

"Yea, whatever." I went back to watching this old lady touch on Lodi.

"Um, do you have to have your hand so close to his, you know?" I said pointing to her hand that was in the crease between his leg and his balls.

"Yes, I do, honey. I've been doing this for 20 years, I know what I'm doing. You just sit over there and be pretty," she said without giving me eye contact.

"I thought he fired you, you're supposed to be checking on me anyway."

"Ladonis fires me every session we have, when I don't allow him to have his way. I'm not fired until he can show me that he can walk without pain."

"Joann, I'm fine. It doesn't matter what you say, I'm walking out that door. Try and stop me," Lodi said. Joann looked at him for a minute and then stood up from her kneeling position, and pushed down on Lodi's hip, which caused him to scream out in pain.

"That was 140 pounds of pressure being pushed on you. Now imagine what's going to happen if you put your 200 and something pounds on these weak hips?"

"Why did I just hear my baby scream?" Mrs. Dawson asked, coming into the living room.

"Because he's hardheaded and won't let me do my job," Joann said.

"Ya job is to help my baby, not hurt him. I hear him scream again then I'm gonna have to hurt you," Mrs. Dawson said, sitting down next to me and handing me another bottle of water. Joann ignored her, which was the best thing she could do. Arguing with Mrs. Dawson was an all-day battle.

"How's my little grand doing in there?" she asked, rubbing on my stomach. When Lodi told her that I was pregnant, she was elated. She hasn't stopped rubbing my belly since we've been here in this house. We decided that we would hold off the engagement news until everything died down and we were back in Jersey.

After Lodi moved me out the hospital, everyone decided it was safer to bring everyone up to Suffern, New York, where he had this huge ass house that no one knew about. He said he was thinking about renting it out but hasn't made a decision just yet.

"The baby is fine, Mrs. Dawson."

"Stop calling me Mrs. Dawson, it's momma to you now. You have my grandbaby inside your tummy. Ladonis, I can't believe you kept this a secret from me for so long."

"Don't start, Ma," Lodi said, getting up off the floor and putting his shoes back on.

"Your leaving, babe?" I asked him.

"Yea. I have to go back and meet Loc and Jay and a few of the guys back in Jersey. I'll be back later," he said, kissing me on the forehead.

"Tell ya sister I would like to see her. She can't avoid me forever. I would use my key to her house but I'm scared what I might walk into," Momma Dawson said, giving Mila a side look.

"Aight, Ma, I'll see y'all later." Lodi waved bye before he left out the door. The room got quiet, awkwardly quiet.

"Momma Dawson, I really like your blouse, is that Versace?" Jamila asked. Momma Dawson side eyed Jamila again.

"Close, sweetie. It's Dior, and my name is Mrs. Dawson to you. You're not pregnant with my grandchild." Jamila sat there with her mouth open as Momma Dawson got up and left the living room.

"That old bat," Jamila said, still sitting there with her mouth open.

"She doesn't seem to like you much, huh?" Joann asked.

"She just mad because her daughter isn't turning out to be the daughter she wanted. Maybe she needs someone to turn her stuck up ass out to bring her back to reality."

"She'll get over it. I'm going to go upstairs and call my husband. Venus, sweetie, how you feeling?" Joann asked.

"I'm good. If I need you I'll let you know. Enjoy your night."

"Come on. Prego/ Let's go watch a movie in that big ass movie theater downstairs," Jamila said, helping me off the couch.

"I'll get the popcorn and meet you down there."

"Ok, don't get lost again in this big ass house. I'm telling you, this is going to be your house one day, Lodi just ain't telling you. He gonna wait until you drop that baby then he gone drop 50 grand on an engagement ring and then drop the keys to this house in the palm of your hand. You just wait and see."

"Yeah, yeah, yeah, whatever."

LODI

I hopped on Highway 202 to meet Loc and Jay. For the last five days, I'd been driving back and forth to the house out in Suffern where Venus and my mom were, and back to Jersey with Loc and Jay. My pops had some business to handle out of town, so he couldn't stay out there with them. I just decided to make the trips back and forth. It was only a half an hour trip so I didn't mind; plus, I was enjoying the nights, sleeping next to Venus.

Somehow, Trub and his crew were able to find out where my parents lived, but by the time they got there, I had already got my parents out of there. They broke in and ransacked the place, but what they weren't expecting was for the neighborhood police to show up so soon. There was a big shoot out which resulted in two officers being shot. The neighborhood video cameras caught their faces, so now they're all in hiding somewhere. We had a few niggas watching the places they frequent, but there's been no sight of Trub and his main crew. If they weren't going to come to us voluntarily, we were gonna make them come to us.

"Yo?" I answered my phone.

"Bro, how far are you? I think we just spotted Mother Goose," Jay said.

"Who the hell is Mother Goose?"

"The old lady that they call Ma Dukes."

"Alright, I'm like 10 minutes away. Keep an eye on that old woman, I heard she carries heat."

"Aight, hurry up and get here or we going in without you." I hung up the phone and got off the Garden State Parkway and on to Highway 80.

LOC

"Where that crippled nigga at?" I asked Jay.

"He said he 10 minutes away. I think we should move in now before his ass gets here. We don't need him slowing us down and you know his stubborn ass ain't about to voluntarily sit out," Jay said, loading the Uzi.

"Agreed," I said, hopping out the car. I waved for Stu, Pop and West to get out their car. We all pulled our masks down as we rounded the gate to the entrance of the projects. It was dark out so no one seen us coming until it was too late. The five of us started laying niggas out left and right. That wasn't our plan but when they started blasting at us, we started blasting back. Eventually, they all started to disperse, leaving us free to roam. One of the niggas we shot wasn't down for the count, so I walked over to him to see what information I could get out of him.

"What apartment does Ma Dukes live in?" I asked him.

"Fuck you, nigga."

"Fuck me? You know you have a chance of living but I can change all that with one bullet to ya dome, nigga. Now, answer my question, which apartment do she live in?"

"What does it matter? Ma Dukes is probably out the back door by now after hearing you fucks blasting."

"You probably right. Yo West, go to the back door; she might be trying to get away. What apartment she lives in?"

"It's 4H," he answered.

"Thanks, nigga," I said before finishing him off with one straight to his dome.

"Stu and Jay, go around to the back with West just in case niggas try to run up on him. Pop and I are gonna go check the apartment out."

"We got in the building and it was quiet, almost too quiet. We took the stairs up to the fourth floor. When we got up there, we found apartment H. I raised my foot and kicked down the door, and a gush of fire came straight at our face. We ducked for cover as the fire continued to flame on.

"This had to be some kind of setup or something. Let's get the fuck up out here."

JAY

In the back of the building, we spotted Ma Dukes running in her platform shoes towards the back parking lot. The three of us chased her down, thinking she was eventually going to give up, but she didn't. She ran as fast as she could in her platform shoes that looked as if they should have had gold fish in them.

She ran over to a long ass station wagon as she ran around to the hatch back that had come open. We ran up closer to her until she jumped from behind the car with a nail gun and started shooting the shit at us.

"What the fuck? This old hag trying to nail our asses to the damn ground," West said. We all started ducking and diving out the way of the flying nails. I heard someone scream and I looked over at Pops, who was on the ground pulling a nail from out this leg.

"Somebody tackle the old hag," I yelled. I was hiding behind the car when I looked up at the building and I saw flames coming from out one of the windows. *What the fuck is going on up there?* I thought to myself, as I looked up at the window that now had flames pouring from it. I knew it was only a matter of time before the fire trucks, followed by the police, would be surrounding the building.

"Yo, tackle that old hag," I said, ducking behind the cars from the flying nails.

"I might break that bitch back if I tackle her," Wes said from behind a car across from me. I was checking my gun for bullets when I heard the air from the tire start to go out, then one side of the car started to lower.

"This heffa really trying to crucify us," I said, peeking my head from behind the car. She had stopped shooting and was now running towards the back of the projects. I pulled up my sweats and took off after her. I had to give it to her, she was really getting it in the platforms. When I caught up to her, I tackled her to the ground and we both went rolling down the hill and came to a stop in the fire lane with me on top of her.

"Ya old ass was determined to get away. You was running like ya pimp was chasing ya ass down," I said, picking her up off the ground. She tried to snatch away from me but I grabbed her by the back of her shirt and pulled her back towards me like she was a dog on a leash. She reached around and smacked the living shit out of me. I stumbled a little, seen a few stars, but I recovered quickly.

"Bitch, you must've lost ya damn mind. Who the fuck you think you smacking like that?" I said, returning the smack which laid her boney ass out like she had just caught the holy ghost. I picked her up over my shoulder and carried her back up the hill.

"Damn, she left her hand print on ya face, dog," West said.

"Shut the fuck up and let's get out of here. Where Loc at?"

"I don't know, they ain't come down here yet."

"Shit, maybe they at the car already. Can you run or do you need West to throw you over his shoulder like a bitch?" I asked Pops. He gave me the finger and stood up. We ran back around the building towards the entrance we came through. Just as we were about to exit through the gate, I heard footsteps coming up behind us. With my gun drawn, I turned around and it was Loc and Stu.

"What the hell happened up there?" I asked Loc.

"I'll tell y'all when we get in the car," he said running next to me. When we got to the truck, I opened the back door and tossed Ma Dukes in. I jumped in the passenger side and Loc pulled off. We were all riding down Main Street when we saw Lodi. He busted a U-turn and started following us.

LODI

I was right around the corner when I spotted Loc's truck speeding down Main Street like someone was chasing his ass, but no one was behind him but Stu's car. This nigga was really asking to be pulled over. I bust a U-turn and started following them. I wasn't sure what the fuck was going on, but I couldn't wait to find out.

They drove for about a good 15 minutes, until we turned off McCarter Highway and into the parking lot of some abandoned warehouse. They all got out the car and so did I.

"What the fuck we doing here and what happened back there?"

"We went in without ya crippled ass," Loc said.

"What you mean y'all went in without me? I told y'all I was 10 minutes away."

"Yeah, well ya crippled ass would have slowed us down, so to avoid that, we went in without you. But all is well because we got the old lady," Loc said, opening the back door of his truck.

"What the fuck happened to her?"

"The bitch smacked the spit out my mouth, so I laid her ass out." I shook my head.

"Where are we and why are we here?"

"Camilla told me about this place. You know sis be hooking me up. Her and Troy owns this place."

Stu came over and got the lady out the car, as the four of us walked into the building. Stu had jumped out on the highway and

153

got in with Loc and Jay, and West took Pops to the emergency room for his leg.

When we got in the big room, there were ropes and chains and shit on the walls. It looked like someone's personal torture chamber. It probably was crazy ass Camilla's torture palace.

"So what we doing with this bitch?" Jay asked, as Stu sat her in the chair and started tying her arms and legs to the chair.

"We about to ransom her ass off. Where her pocketbook?" Loc asked. Jay handed him the pocketbook and he went inside and pulled out her cellphone. He started taking pictures of her tied up to the chair.

"Now let's send these out. Son number one and son number two. I wonder which one is Trub. Oh well, I'll send it to both of them," he said with a smile.

TRUB

"Fuck, fuck, fuck," I said slamming my phone into the steering wheel of my truck.

"I thought you told Ma Dukes to stay her ass in the suite until this shit was settled?"

"I did, but you know her ass stubborn as hell. You know she's too attached to that fuckin' apartment to leave it even for a damn night," Peabo said.

"Shit, man. I guess it's eye for a motherfuckin' eye then," I said, staring at the house that Lodi had been coming and going from. One of my little niggas spotted him riding through the city on some King Jaffe, like he was untouchable. I could have had him finish his ass up, but I wanted to know where he was keeping Mars. We had run through all of their houses and had niggas sitting and watching them shits, but none of their asses came home. We even had the mother and father house under watch, and the dike bitch shawty was being watched too.

When little homie spotted Lodi, he followed him to this house and been sitting here, watching him leave this house in Suffern numerous times.

I hopped out the car and everyone did the same thing. Guns cocked and ready for war, it was about eight of us hopping over the fence. We started surrounding the big house, looking for any possible entryway. Even if we had to blow a fucking hole through the wall, we were getting our asses in that bitch.

VENUS

"Hey, Mama Dawson, we were all downstairs about to watch a movie. You want to come join us?" I asked her as I peeked my head into her temporary bedroom.

"It depends on which movie we watching," she said.

"Well, we're on the fence between *What's Love Got to Do With It* and *Sparkle*."

"Well, I hope everybody chooses Sparkle," she said, getting up off the bed and putting on her silk robe.

"See, that's how I know this was meant to be, but no, it's a tie now. We may have to flip a coin," I said to her.

"No coin flip needed, *Sparkle* it is," she concluded.

"We're going to start the movie in five minutes. Come downstairs when you're ready," I said, leaving out the room.

Forty-five minutes into the movie, Mrs. Dawson and I was up performing "Giving Him Something He Can Feel" as it was being done on the movie. When I tell her that EnVogue was my favorite girl group, she called me a bull-shitter until I started listing all the songs and I even performed "Don't Let Go" for her.

After the movie, we played a game of Charades. It was Mrs. Dawson and I against Joanne and Jamila. We were kicking their butts. Mrs. Dawson was such a competitive person; she even broke out in a twerk when we won.

"I can't wait to tell your son about you," I said to her.

"And what he gon' do? That's how he got here," she

responded.

I was slowly falling in love with this woman. She would have made a great mom and role model to a daughter.

"This was fun y'all, but I'm about to turn in to bed," Jamila said.

"Yea, I think we all about tired." We all left out the basement and was heading upstairs to the bedrooms, when the house alarms started going off.

"What the hell is that?" Jamila asked.

"The house alarm," I said, running over to the wall panels and pushing it open so that I could turn on the monitor. I watched as people dressed in all black were jumping over the fence.

"Oh shit, who the fuck are they?" I looked harder into the screen trying to make out some of their faces, but could only recognize one for some reason.

"I think that's the guy Trub. The one Mars been with," I said in a low voice feeling myself start to panic.

"And who the hell is Trub and Mars?" Mrs. Dawson questioned.

"You know that guy right there. I saw you in a picture with him," Joann stated.

I pulled out my phone with tears now running from my eyes from fear, and at the same time, guilt. This was all my fault. I should have kept my crazy ass away from Lodi and his family. Maybe I should have stayed in Edna where everyone could have remained safe without my presence.

Lodi's phone started ringing and he answered on the second ring.

"I know, baby. I got the alarm hooked up to my phone, we on our way."

"Ok, how long?" I asked him.

"Probably about 20 minutes but I'm going to try and get there as fast as I can. Aye, put Jamila on the phone." I handed the phone over to her.

"What's up, L?" she answered calmly. I don't know what he was saying to her because all she did was shake her head up and down followed by 'mm hmms' and 'oks'. She handed me back my phone just as someone started kicking at the front door.

"Come on," Mila said, grabbing my arm and pulling me with her. Mrs. Dawson and Joann followed us as we went back down to the basement. Mila shut the doors and went over to the breaker box and cut out all the power to the house.

"Lodi said they'll be here in 20 minutes. We just need to stay down here until they get here."

"So does anyone wanna tell me what's going on and who them people are?" Mrs. Dawson asked.

"They're after me, Momma Dawson. When you didn't see me for those few months, I was with them and now I think they're back for me."

"Oh my God. Well, it'll be over my dead body if they think they pulling you up out of here," she said, gathering all of her thin long hair and twisting it into a bun, and then picking up one of the elephant statues that was on the side table. This preppy lady was ready for war.

TRUB

"Circle around the back, check all the doors and windows. These niggas got Ma Dukes and we ain't leaving without a body, preferably Mars," I called to the guys, as they all scattered in different directions. I stood at the front door, attempting to kick the shit down. If the iron gates to the driveway weren't closed, I would have bust through this shit with my truck.

I picked up one of the lawn chairs and attempted to bust the window, but that shit ain't do nothing. It didn't even put a chip in the window. The damn chair bounced right back in my hands. They must've had some kind of protective glass on the windows.

"Man, we ain't getting in this bitch," Peabo said, giving up. I could tell his head wasn't in this shit with everything that was going on with Lynea and now Ma Dukes. His head was probably all fucked up at the moment.

"There's a way in this bitch, bro, we just got to be patient," I said to him.

"Man, by the time we find a way in, them niggas will be back. You know what, I'm going back to find Ma Dukes. Somebody in the 'jects had to see something."

"Aight, man. You go and let me know what's going on. I promise I'll get Ma Dukes back, and get those niggas back for this." We hugged one another as he ran off. I turned back to the door just as the lights went out.

I continued to kick at the doorknob on the front door when

161

someone inside started unlocking the shit. I pulled out my gun as the door flung open. It was Nutz.

"How the fuck you get in here?" I asked him.

"Back door was left unlocked," he said.

"Ain't that something? Search the house, someone is in here somewhere." After everyone came into the house, we started tearing the shit up. Ripping down pictures, pulling TVs off the walls, flipping couches and beds. The house was big as hell. It seemed as if we would be searching forever until I heard a woman scream. I followed the screams which led down to the basement. Deez had two of the women, one pinned against the wall and another by the hair, as she swung at him with an elephant. The older woman was able to tag Deez in the nose with the elephants, causing it to start leaking blood.

"Come get one of these broads, man," he called with his head held towards the ceiling to keep the blood from leaking. One of the other guys ran over and tried to get a hold of the woman, but she swung the elephant at him, hitting him in the head, laying the nigga out on the ground. This woman was lethal with that fucking elephant.

"Fuck this shit," I said, aiming my gun at her with my finger on the trigger. A sharp pain in my back caused me to fire aimlessly at the wall unit against the wall, causing it to start wobbling before falling. I felt another pain which brought me to my knees. I reached in my back and tried to pull whatever it was out my back, when someone's knee came across my face. I dropped my gun.

The dark-skinned girl came around and picked up my gun and held it to my head.

"You niggas get the fuck out the house or I'm blowing his head off," the dark-skinned chick said with the gun to my head. Without hesitation, Deez let the two women go that he had and ran over to help me up. Nutz also came and helped me up. They started walking backwards towards the steps. I guess they weren't moving fast enough because the chick shot at our feet.

I looked her right in her eyes because I was going to kill this bitch if I ever ran into her again. We backpedaled out the room and up the stairs.

"We really about to bitch out and run, nigga? Because of some bitch?" Deez said, dropping me on the lawn.

"Nigga, pick me the fuck up and get me to the car. You know what, I'll walk myself. Go shut them doors and barricade all them bitches in," I demanded.

"Even Mars?"

"I didn't see her in there," I answered.

"Nigga, she was standing over by the wall unit that you shot at." I sat there thinking for a minute.

"Let's just go," I said. We were all walking back to the gate when it started opening and four cars came racing in.

"Shit," I said as the bullets started firing. I tried my best to run as fast as I could to the fence, but the stab wound to my back was preventing me from moving as fast as I could. I looked behind me and one of the cars came driving toward us. We all took off to the fence as the car shifted directions and was now heading towards the fence. D-Mack and Chops stood there helping me get over the fence. When the car came towards us, they left me hanging on the fence as they ran in the other direction. The car ran straight into the fence and I fell on top of the hood. It backed up and then started driving forward in the direction D-Mack and Chops ran. Chops fat ass wasn't going too fast. I'm honestly shocked that he got over the fence in the beginning. Whoever was driving the car pressed on the gas and ran into him, and he came flying on to the hood, hitting me, causing us both to fall off the car. The car door opened and that nigga Lodi stepped out the car. He came limping over to me as I started crawling away. Chops was lying on the lawn unconscious.

"You chose the wrong nigga's girl to fuck with," he said, coming closer to me.

"I didn't choose her, she chose me. Remember that, nigga."

"She ain't choose you, her subconscious chose you. I bet you ain't know what you were getting yourself into, huh? You should have just let me walk away with her that night she stepped to you. Now look you, about to die over a ghost that will no longer exist. I got the real one, I got the one that matters," he said.

"Oh yeah? Well, have fun raising my seed, motherfucker. I been busting in that pussy for almost five months now," I bragged. I loved seeing that angry look on his face. It really made this moment worth it.

"Kiss my baby for me," I said before there was a flash.

LODI

I stood over Trub as I watched the smoke from my gun evaporate into the air. Getting rid of this nigga once and for all felt great. Felt like I had just accomplished a goal that was set years ago. When I looked up, the other niggas were fleeing in their car. They weren't even going to check and see if their boy was dead, they just bounced. A bunch of pussies.

"Yo L, we got a problem," I heard Jay call from the entrance of the house.

I walked as fast as my fucked up hips allowed me, until I made it in the house. I followed Jay down the stairs to the basement where the movie theater was. I noticed everyone surrounding Venus as she laid on the floor next to the fallen wall unit.

"What happened?" I yelled as I got closer to her.

"The wall unit fell on top of her. She's unconscious and she just started bleeding," Jamila said. I look down between her legs and it was blood coming down her pink pajama pants. I began to panic.

"Call the ambulance," I said. My mother immediately jumped up and ran over to the house phone. I got down on my knees next to Venus and started stroking her face.

"Venus, baby, wake up," I called, but nothing. My mind started racing as I continued to try and wake her. I don't know what it is about us trying to have a baby, but it seems like it just wasn't going to happen for us. Maybe we weren't meant to be parents together. Maybe this was God's way of trying to protect the baby from Venus's mental disorder.

"They're on their way, honey," my mom mentioned as she ran back over to me.

"Don't worry. It's all going to be ok, sweetie."

"I know, Ma. Someone help me carry her to the car. The ambulance is going to take too long to get here. I can drive over there myself by the time they arrive." I picked up her head and Jay ran over and picked up her legs.

"Ladonis, honey, I don't think you should do that. You don't know what you can be messing up by moving her. Let's just leave her still," my mom suggested.

I wasn't listening. Jay and I carried her upstairs to the car that was parked in the middle of the lawn. Just as soon as we were about to open the car door and put her in, the ambulance came into the driveway.

"Over here," I yelled.

"Wait, bro," Jay said giving me a head nod towards Trub's body that was still sitting in front of the car.

"Shit. Alright. Help me bring her to the ambulance and you go back and move the body." We both hurried Venus to the ambulance. They opened the back of the truck and instructed us to get in and lay her on the gurney. We gently laid her down and Jay jumped back out the ambulance. They started checking her vitals and everything, and then noticed the blood between her legs.

"We need to get her to the ER immediately. Sir, are you

coming? If not, you need to exit the vehicle now because we need to go," one of the EMT people said.

"I'm coming with y'all," I replied, as I sat down in the corner and out of their way.

As they were working on her, her eyes started to flutter as if she was trying to open them.

"She's waking up," I said to the EMT. He stood up and started checking her vitals again. Venus's eyes popped open. She looked lost and confused. I reached over and grabbed her hand.

"Lodi," she said, looking over at me.

"Yea, it's me, V, baby."

"What's going on?" she asked as she winced in pain.

"There's something going on with the baby."

"Not again," she said as she yelled out in pain.

VENUS

It didn't take them long to get me out of the back of ambulance. I was immediately rushed to labor and delivery. The doctor said I need an emergency C-section or the baby could kill me. They wouldn't allow Lodi to come in the back with me, as much as he begged and pleaded. After a while, he was told that he had to stand back and couldn't get in their way. All of this really had me scared, as I screamed out in pain once again. At this moment, I made a promise to myself that this would be the last time I get pregnant. I didn't understand how a moment that was meant to be so joyous was filled with so much pain and despair.

I was placed in some kind of hospital gown and was rolled into the OR. Lodi followed behind, holding my trembling hand. They placed a mask over my face and all I remember was looking into Lodi's eyes before I slowly fell asleep.

LODI

"While I was outside, the doctor informed me that judging by the size of the baby, Venus had to be about five months pregnant, which was a bittersweet moment for me. Sweet because it restored my faith that the baby was indeed mine, and bitter because the baby was nowhere near close being ready to be born. I asked what did it mean for the baby; would the baby be able to survive being born so early? She said that it has happened before. The baby will have to be in the hospital for some time before he was ready to go out in the world.

The C-section started. Standing in the back of the operating room, I was still able to see enough that made me want to pass out. I watched them cut into Venus's stomach and once they had access, the doctor pulled out a handful of baby with one hand, and held him in the palm of her hand. Looking at the tiny baby, I wanted to cry because I felt so bad. How could my first child be brought into the world under such circumstances? Maybe all this shit was my fault. Maybe it was some form of karma for all the shit that I'd done when I was younger. I prayed to God that if he allowed both Venus and the baby to come out of this alive and safe, that I would start changing my ways in life.

I was able to go inside the intensive care unit and see my son, but I couldn't stay for long seeing him hooked up to all the machines and wires and shit. I left out the room and into the hallway to catch my breath, as a tear rolled down my face. I wiped it away and went to find out where they were taking Venus.

They had finally brought her back to the room about an hour ago. I sat at her bedside waiting for her to wake up. I called my family that was waiting downstairs and told them that they could leave and I would call them when she woke up. My mother wasn't trying to hear that, but with a little coercion, she finally left with Jay and Jamila. Loc had taken Joann home and said he was going to come back up here since he had nowhere to be. I took out my phone and started reading about Huey Newton: Spirit of the Panther, as I waited for Venus to wake up. I looked up from my phone for a quick second and a familiar face walked by the door. I stood up and walked over to the door.

"Kim," I called to her. She looked a little thicker from behind and her hair had grown out a little, but enough to put in a ball on the top of her head. She turned around and her face was still as beautiful as ever, but her belly was now big and round. She looked shocked to see me and almost hesitant.

"Hello Ladonis," she said with a smile.

"How you been, Kim?" I said, walking up to her and giving her a hug.

"I been good and pregnant," she said.

"I see, congratulations Ma. How far along are you?"

"Nine months, Ladonis. Any day now, this little guy will be here."

"Nine months? Damn, girl, you work fast," I said.

"What do you mean by that? I work fast?" she asked.

"Meaning, we broke up like nine, ten months ago and you already pregnant by the next nigga. But look, that's neither here nor there. You look beautiful, Kim."

She sat there staring at me for a minute before her face turned to a scowl.

"Pregnant by the next nigga, Lodi? Really? You know I'm not even like that. You are the nigga I'm pregnant by, but I tried not to bother you with it seeing as though you're happy with that crazy chick. Ain't no next nigga, but since you wanna act like a dick before even doing the math in your head, you are the father, my nigga. I'm down for whatever DNA testing you want. Fuck that, I'll even go to Maury with yo ass. How about you come see me in a month when the baby is born so we can get the whole DNA testing thing that I know you're thinking about right now, out the way."

I stood there just staring at her.

"Alright, I'll see you in a month then," I said, walking away stunned and unable to speak. I looked back and Kim was no longer standing there. I leaned against the wall and took in a deep breath. *What the fuck just happened?* I asked myself. In a matter of hours, I went from no kids to possibly two. Why the fuck would Kim keep this shit away from me? I was going to kill her ass once she dropped that baby. I would have never allowed her to go through this pregnancy alone.

"Shit," I said aloud as I ran my hand down my face. *How was I going to tell Venus?*

"Lodi," I heard her soft voice call from the room. I walked into the room and her eyes were wide open.

"V, baby, how you feeling?" I asked her.

"Dizzy and numb," she answered.

"Damn, that sounds like a good time to me." She laughed.

"It is, how is the baby?" she asked.

"Uh, he's alive, V. We just have to pray that he continues to get better.

Honestly, it's not looking good, but he has two strong parents so he's going to make it, I promise."

She started crying.

"What did we do so wrong that our baby has to pay?" she cried.

"We didn't do anything wrong. We just been putting ourselves in bad situations, but that's all over now. It's about us and our baby," I said, reaching down and kissing her on her forehead.

"Let me see if one of the nurses can take you in to see him."

Two Days Later

"Come on, baby, we have to leave now. The doctor is on his way to examine you. We'll be back later for his next feeding," I said, trying to convince Venus to leave her newborn baby. I knew it was hard for her, it was hard for me too, but us hovering over him wasn't going to make him get better any faster.

"Bye, baby," she said, kissing the top of the incubator. Our baby boy only weighed one pound eleven ounces. The baby couldn't leave until he had gained at least five more pounds. By the way things were looking, that might not happen for a while. He was barely eating anything and I had to admit, the shit was scaring the hell out of me.

I helped Venus back into her wheelchair. I myself should have been in a damn wheelchair. I wasn't at my best yet, but I was getting there. A few more sessions with Joann, I should be good.

I rolled her back to her recovery room and helped her into the bed, just as the doctor knocked on the door and walked right in.

"Miss Morgan, how are feeling?" the doctor asked, walking into the room.

"Sore. Can I have some more of those pain meds I was getting?"

"Sure, I'll let the nurse know," she said, lifting Venus's gown up and checking her C-section incision.

"Your stitches are healing well. There is a little redness but it'll go away. Try to refrain from bending or any form of stretching," she said, putting Venus's gown back down.

"When will she be able to go home?" I asked.

"She'll be well enough to go home tomorrow."

"What about the baby?" Venus asked.

"Well, the baby can't leave for some time. I can't give you an exact date, but before the baby can leave he has to gain more weight and he has to start eating on his own. Have you two chosen a name for the little guy?" the doctor asked.

"Yes, LJ," Venus answered.

"What does LJ stand for?"

"Ladonis Jr."

"Nice. Ok, I'll be back to check on you tomorrow before you go. Enjoy your evening," she said before leaving the room.

"Come lay with me, Ladonis," she demanded. I kicked off my shoes and climbed in the bed and cuddled up against her. She started looking for something to watch on TV, but there was nothing, so we just settled on the news.

I started getting lost in my thoughts. My thoughts of the baby's wellbeing, the fact that we still haven't told anyone but Loc about the engagement, me getting back to a hundred percent, and the fact that I still haven't told Venus about Kim's baby. I figured I would wait until the baby was born and we do the DNA test. *Why stress her out over something that may not be?* I was brought out of my dreams by a knock on the door. I looked up and there were two detectives at the door.

"How can we help you, gentlemen?" I asked.

"Ma'am, are you Venus Morgan?" one of them questioned Venus.

"Yes, I am; how can I help you?" she responded.

"Would you happen to know someone by the name of Mars Morgan? I'm assuming you do seeing as though the two of you look identical and have the same last name," the detective said, holding out a picture of Mars on a boat.

"Well, you know what they say when you assume things, right? You make an ass out of yourself."

"I doubt if I'm making an ass out of myself at this moment. Is this your twin sister?"

"Yes, she is her sister, why are you asking about her?" I asked now in full lawyer mode.

"This woman here in the photo is a suspect in the death of Marcia Hunt. She was pushed off a boat two months ago. We questioned a few people and they recall an altercation between Mars and Ms. Hunt moments before Ms. Hunt was pushed overboard."

"Ok, and?"

"So we need to question her, but there seems to be no trace of her anywhere. All traces of her leads back to you. You say the two of you are twin sisters?"

"Yeah, something like that," Venus answered.

"What do you mean something like that?"

"She means they didn't grow up together and she sees her every now and then," I spoke up for Venus.

"Excuse me, sir, who are you?"

"Her fiancé and her lawyer," I responded.

"Why does she need a lawyer? We're just looking for answers."

"She doesn't need one, but it's a good thing I'm here."

"How do we know you're not Mars pretending to be Venus?"

"That's bullshit, get the fuck out."

"No problem, lawyer, but we will be looking into your background. Digging up dirt on this Mars person," the detective stated.

"You do that. Now, if you don't mind, get to stepping," I said as one of the detectives handed me his card before he left out the door. I followed behind them to make sure they were gone before I shut the room door.

"Shit," I said.

"What the fuck?" Venus shouted, catching me off guard.

"Don't worry, V, baby. My father is one of the best lawyers around and he had connections in many places. We'll handle this, you just worry about getting better. I'll be back later on tonight to sleep with you."

VENUS

After Ladonis left out the room, I jumped out the bed in search of my cellphone. I couldn't go back to Edna. I was a mother now. I didn't deserve to be in jail again for something Mars's ass did again. This was a never ending situation. Mars starts some shit and I'm left to pay the consequences.

"Mila, it's me," I said into my phone.

"I know it's you, crazy, I have caller ID," she responded.

"I need your help, Mila. I need you to do something for me. More so with me."

"Anything, girl, you know you're my baby."

I sat on the phone running my plan down to her as the tears fell down my eyes. In my head, this was my only solution if I didn't want to be locked away again.

LODI

"Pop, I need you to do this for me," I said to my father who was sitting across from me. I had just asked him to help me get Venus out of this situation. I explained to him everything that was going on with her condition and the whole situation.

"Does she have records to back it up? A therapist? A doctor?" my father asked.

"Yeah, she does. Uh, Dr. Burke is his name."

"Good, we can get any records he may have on her."

"She was also telling me about a video they have of her switching into her alter personality."

"That's good. I need all of that because once they find out that she's not a twin then they'll surely come looking for her and they will arrest her. We need to be prepared."

"You right. I'll get on it, Pop," I said getting up and leaving out the house. My first stop was Dr. Burke's office.

Pulling up to his office, I tried calling Venus's cellphone but she wasn't answering. I'm guessing she was sleeping. I put the phone in my pocket and got out the car and started walking towards the office. When I walked inside the building, a super chipper lady with rosy cheeks jumped up out of her seat.

"Hey, I'm looking for Dr. Burke," I said to her.

"Dr. Burke transferred. We have Dr. Colins now. Would you like to schedule an appointment with Dr. Colins, sir?" she asked.

"No, I need Dr. Burke. How would I be able to get a hold of a certain patient of Dr. Burke's?"

"Well, I would need permission from the patient to release their medical records to you."

"Look, Miss, I need these records now. I don't have time to get her permission. This is in no way to harm her; this is to help her. Ms. Morgan is in a little bit of trouble and I'm one of the lawyers who is going to help her get out of trouble."

"Wait, Ms. Morgan? As in Venus Morgan?" the woman asked.

"Yes, Venus Morgan, ma'am."

"Oh, poor dear. Is she ok?"

"She is, but she won't be if I don't get those records." She sat there for a minute and I could see the concern all over her face.

"I'm sorry. I will get in trouble if I give you those records without permission. I stored all of Dr. Burke's records in the basement. As soon as you get that release form signed by Ms. Morgan, I can supply you with what you need. We close at six and the guard leaves at seven, so you can come back in the morning with Ms. Morgan's signature," she said, winking her eye. I wasn't catching on at first, but then I figured it out. I said bye to her before I left out the building. I sat in my car thinking of my next move, before pulling out my phone.

"Yo, black man," I said when Moore answered the phone.

"What's good with you my boy? It's good to see you doing good," Moore said.

"Shit, I'm dealing with a problem. What happened to them tapes I asked you for?" I questioned. A while ago when Venus first told me about the video of her pushing some girl in the street, I had got in touch with Moore so that he could get those tapes for me.

"I been had them. I got my hands on them after you were hit. I been holding on to them for you."

"That's good, Moore, I knew I fucked with you for a reason. Where can I meet you to get them?"

"Meet me at K-mart in Elmwood Park. I'll be there in 20 minutes," he said, hanging up the phone, and I made my way to meet him.

LOC

"Ma, come meet me, I need you," I said on the phone to Joann.

"Oh really, you need big momma, huh? What you need me for, baby boy?"

"You damn right I need you. I need you to come help me release some of this pinned up frustration."

"Mmm, that sounds like a good time, baby boy. Unfortunately, I can't meet you right now, he's here."

"Fuck that nigga, be out, ma. He won't notice you missing, he doesn't pay attention to yo' ass any way."

"Watch ya mouth now, you have no rights commenting on my marriage."

"Who's that on the phone, Jo?" I heard someone ask in the background.

"No one, baby. Just someone trying to sell something again," she answered.

"Again? Give me this phone. Who is this?" the guy asked getting on the phone.

"Uhhh, this is Jake from State Farm," I said fucking with him.

"State Farm? Look, we're pretty satisfied with Nationwide. Please take us off your contact list," the dumb ass said.

"Yes, sir," I continued to play along with him until the phone hung up. After I hung up the phone, I sent her a text telling her to make some time for me or I was popping up at her crib and dragging her out the house. I put the phone down and just started driving with no destination in mind. I ended up all the way on the other side of town where I spotted Trub's little dumb ass minions Deez, Nutz and Don Don. I was bored so I figured I would fuck with them niggas. I circled around the block, reached under the chair and pulled out my Uzi. I rolled down the window and started spraying bullets at them. They all started running in different directions. I followed the one that was running the slowest which was Don Don. I felt like I was in a game of Black Ops, as I pulled over and lined him up in the crosshairs. I fired, lighting his legs up. I wasn't shooting to kill, just to put him down.

"Riccckkkyyyyy," I yelled imitating the scene from *Boys in the Hood*, making myself laugh. I pulled my gun back in the car and sped off looking for the other two. I circled the neighborhood a few times and couldn't find them, so I bounced.

I continued to wander around aimlessly until I decided to just go check Jay. I arrived at her house just as Jamila rushed out the house.

"Damn, where you in a rush to?" I asked her.

"Oh, hey Loc, Jay isn't here right now," she said out of breath, carrying a big ass duffle bag.

"Where that nigga at?"

"Uh, I don't know, call her," she said pushing past me and heading to her car.

"Where you going, Jamila?"

"To the laundry. If you speak to her tell her I love her," she said before hopping in her car and speeding off, leaving me standing there.

LODI

I looked down at the video tapes I had in my hand and thanked God for these. I wasn't sure what was on them, only the details that Venus had already shared with me. I just hoped this was going to help her be cleared from what charges they were going to hit her with. I put the tapes under the front seat chair. I cut my car off and pulled my hoodie over my head. I grabbed the crowbar off the front seat and walked over to the front door of the building. I sat there for about five minutes trying to jimmy the lock. I finally got the door open and the building's alarm went off. I immediately went looking around for the basement door. When I found the basement door, I ran down the stairs and started searching through the boxes. It felt like I was down there forever until I found the box that was labeled Venus Morgan, 2008-2015. I grabbed the whole box and ran up the stairs and out the door. When I got to the parking lot, I could hear the sirens coming down the block as I dodged through the parking lot to my car. I threw the box in the passenger seat and I hopped in and pulled off out the other side of the parking lot.

I was sitting in my car outside the hospital for about 10 minutes, going through the box that had everything about Venus and Mars. Reading some of the shit was creepy as hell. It was like I was reading a psychological thriller or some shit. Dr. Burke has had two altercations with Mars. One time she tried to staple his hand to the desk, and another time she tried to stab him with a prison made shank. This chick was fucking dangerous and she needed to be in a straitjacket locked behind bars, but that means that Venus would have had to be there too. This was going to be a tough case to fight, but my pops and I were going to fight the shit. I'll be damned if I let Venus go back to jail for some bullshit that she couldn't control. Even if I had to take her and skip town, I was willing to risk it all for my baby girl.

I closed the box and got out the car and went into the hospital. My first stop was to see LJ. I was sure that's where Venus was going to be, seeing as though she couldn't stay away from him. It was his feeding time anyway, so nine times out of ten she was in there.

I dressed in the gown and knocked on the door seeing if it was okay that I entered. She gave me the ok and I walked in. Shockingly, Venus was nowhere to be found.

"How's he doing?" I asked the nurse.

"It's too early to tell, but this little guy is strong; I can tell by his little grip. He's going to be alright," she said.

"Yeah, he's just like his parents. He's a survivor. Has his mom been by?"

"Uh, no, I haven't see her come since the last time the two of you came by."

"Really? That's odd. She's probably sleeping. She did ask the doctor for some more pain meds. I'm going to go check on her. See you later, little guy," I said touching the top of his incubator.

I left out the room and headed towards Venus's room. I walked in the room expecting to see her in bed sleeping, but the bed was empty. I went to check the bathroom and she wasn't there either. *Where the hell is this girl?* I asked myself, sitting down on the bed. There was a piece of paper on the pillow. I picked it up, expecting it to be nothing, but that thought died when I started reading the note.

Dear Ladonis,

I'm sorry to have to leave like this. It pains me to my core to leave without talking to you or being able to take my baby with me. I know you said that you would handle this and I believe that you will try your best, but either way, I don't see this turning out good for me. I need to get far away; I can't go back to jail. I can't continue to pay for the consequences of Mars's actions. I didn't know what else to do but run. I promise, once I figure out where I'm going, I will let you know. Until then, please watch over LJ. I love you beyond this world. I can't wait until the next time I see you. I will continue to hold our last memory until we're together again to create new ones.

Love Forever, Venus

*****

5 Years Later

"Bro, how we know which one is yours?" Peabo asked. Sitting in the driver's seat of the borrowed Ford Explorer.

"Let me see those," I said, grabbing for the binoculars that Peabo had in his hand. I put them to my eyes and looked through them. I watched as the two little boys that couldn't be no more than five years old, played in the front yard of the house whose lawn I was shot in and left for dead. If it wasn't for my brother coming back to check up on me, I would have been dead. Them niggas Deez and Nutz left my ass to die. It was all good because as soon as I recovered, I came back to Jersey and blew both of their brains out.

"It has to be the one in the red shirt. He looks a little like me," I said.

"Let me see," Lynea said, reaching in the front seat for the binoculars.

"Wait, shit. I know I'm right, it's the one in the red shirt," I said, handing Lynea the binoculars so that she could look at the boys."

"I don't know, bro; I think it's the one in the blue shirt. He has light eyes. Didn't you say Mars's eyes turned colors sometimes? Why the hell these two motherfuckers look alike? Did they have another baby?"

"Look, don't call my seed a motherfucker. I'll put ya burnt ass out this damn car," I said.

Lynea was fully recovered from Mars lighting that ass on fire. She just had burn marks that covered about 60 percent of her body. Her face was fine, but her hands, back and legs were burned. She had to remain in the burn unit for a year to recover. When she was finally released to Ma Dukes, she brought her down to Florida where I was staying.

After the nigga shot me, he never checked to see if I was dead for sure. His dike sister dragged me behind the car. After the ambulance pulled off, she and everyone else jumped in the car and left. I felt like I was on the verge of dying. I think I even seen the light at one point. I don't know what told Peabo to turn around, but he did, and that gut instinct of his saved my life.

"Nah, it's the one in the red shirt, I feel that shit in my bones. They just made the biggest mistake by allowing him to play out here alone." I jumped out the car and walked over to the gate.

"Aye, kid," I called, kneeling down below the gate so no one could see me but the kids.

"Kid," I called again and they both turned.

"Red shirt, come here for a minute," I quietly called. The little kid got up and walked towards the gate. When he got there, he sat down in the grass in front of me.

"Hey kid, what's your name?" I asked him.

"Ayden," he replied.

"How old are you Ayden?"

"I'm 4 years old, I'll be five soon."

Yep, it's him, I thought to myself.

"Who's that?" I asked him, pointing to the other little boy in the yard.

"That's my brother, LJ."

"Cool. Look what I got you?" I said, pulling out the toy truck I had picked up from the gas station. I handed it to him.

"You like that?"

"Yes,"

"Who's inside your house?"

"Just my dad?"

"Where's your mom?"

"She's at work," he responded, while pushing the truck back and forth in the grass.

"I'm a friend of your moms. She told me to come take you to get some ice cream, you wanna go?"

"Yes, can my brother come too?"

"Nah, just you little man. Come on," I said standing up. I reached over the iron gate and pulled the boy up and over, and held him on my hip as I crossed the street and headed towards the car.

"Daadddyyy!" I heard the other little boy that was on the lawn yell. I ran to the car and jumped in and Peabo pulled off.

To be continued…

Disturbed: An Unbalanced Love 3

SNEAK PEEK:

He's Nothing Like Them Other Ones:
A Kandi Coated Love Story 2

"Wait, hol' up, hol' up, hol up," I said in the phone, not sure of what I was just hearing.

"Tech, what did you just say?"

"Kandice, John is on his way to the hospital. That bitch, Kori stabbed him up, man. He's going in and out of consciousness. He's lost so much blood, man, shit," Tech cried on the other end of the phone.

"He's convulsing," I heard someone yell in the background.

"Oh my God, Tech, what's going on?" I yelled in the phone.

"Tech!"

"We're losing him, charge to 300," that voice said again. I could hear the beeping from the defibrillator and then the shock.

"Nothing, charge again." By this time, I had tears streaming down my face as I sat in my wheelchair in the middle of the hospital hallway.

"Tech!" I called again and still nothing. A piece of me was deteriorating with every beep from the machine I could hear in the background, then the phone went dead.

"Hello," I said, then removed the phone from my ear and looked at the screen. I had lost service. I quickly turned my wheelchair in the direction of the elevators. My father had taken Kamari to Billy Beez, so there was no one to push me. I had gotten bored of sitting in my room, so I decided to go for a roll around the hospital.

I rolled down the halls of the hospital towards the elevators as fast as I could, as I tried redialing Tech's number, but the call kept dropping. I pushed myself as fast as I could. I felt like I was in the Paralympics the way I was maneuvering through the hall.

"Ma'am, you need to slow down," one of the nurses called, but I ignored her ass and kept on going. I noticed the elevator sign right ahead of me, so I pushed harder, dodging a yellow sign in the middle of the floor. I got closer to the elevator and tried slowing myself down, but the wheels of my wheelchair and these slippery ass floors caused me to slide and then tip over, busting my face on the floor. What made it even worse was that I fell in front of this little boy who had to be about 10 years old. He found the shit hysterical. I shot him an evil look as I used the wall to pick myself and my wheelchair up. I pressed on the elevator button and the door came open. I rolled onto the elevator and turned towards the kid. As the elevator door closed, I stuck out my tongue at him.

I got down to the lobby and went outside. I redialed Tech's number and it went straight to voicemail. I tried again, just as an ambulance was driving by. I used my hands to cover my ears from the sirens, as I waited for Tech to pick up the phone. It went to voicemail.

"Shit," I cursed.

"Tech, pick up the damn phone."

I was about to redial his number when the back doors of the

ambulance burst open and one of the EMS personnel jumped out and started helping remove the gurney from the back. I redialed Tech's number as I watched them roll the gurney out. The doctors came running out of the emergency room doors.

"What do we have?" one of the doctors asked.

"Twenty-four-year-old Korrina Smith, self-inflicted stab wound to the chest. Vitals are stable," the EMS personnel said.

Hearing the name Korrina caught my attention immediately. I quickly hung up the phone and started rolling over there. I knew it was Kori by the healed track marks that became forever permanent on her left arm that hung from the gurney. This wasn't a coincidence.

"Excuse me, sir, was there a guy with her?" I asked the EMT person. He ignored me as he hurried and shut the back of the ambulance, and started walking towards the driver's side. I rolled in his path, getting his attention, causing him to stop in his tracks.

"Was there a man found with the girl?"

"Yes, he's in the other ambulance behind us. Now move out my way, ma'am, I have an emergency to get to," he stated softly, moving me out the way.

I backed up on to the sidewalk and waited for the other ambulance to show up. I was so concerned about John I had completely forgotten that I was outside in a hospital gown. I tried calling Tech again, but just like last time, it went to voicemail.

"Shit," I shouted, just as I heard the faint sounds of a siren. I turned towards the entrance and waited for the ambulance to pull up. Two doctors came out the hospital and stood on the sidewalk and also waited for the ambulance to appear.

A few seconds later, the ambulance came speeding into the entrance and up to the emergency doors. I rolled up to the doors before the hospital staff could get to the door.

"Excuse us, ma'am, we need to get there," the nurse said.

"Oh, sorry," I said, moving out the way. They opened the door and an EMT person jumped out and helped with the gurney. I looked up and saw Tech jumping out next.

"Tech!" I yelled, as they pulled John out of the back of the ambulance. I stood in shock as I looked over his blood soaked body. I could hear them reading off his stats, but I was unable to hear because the sight of the blood was louder than the sound of his voice.

"Kandice, you alright?" Tech asked as I slowly started coming back down to earth.

"What happened?" I questioned.

"Dumb bitch Kori stabbed him 13 times then stabbed herself. I hope she makes it because I'm killing that bitch myself."

"Not before I get to her. I'm feeding that hoe to the sharks. After what she did to me and now John, that bitch deserves to rot in hell."

They started pushing John away and Tech started pushing me towards the hospital entrance. Gunshots started to rang out from behind us and glass from the hospital windows started to shatter.

"Oh shit," Tech said, knocking me to the ground then jumping on top of me. I covered my ears with my hands as the loud shots continued for what felt like hours. When the echoes of the gunshots stopped, I removed my hands just as the car that was shooting pulled off and out of the parking lot.

"Tech," I called, but he didn't answer.

"Tech," I called again. this time nudging him, but he didn't answer nor did he move. Something wasn't right.

To be continued...

Other Releases from Myiesha:

A New Jersey Love Story: Troy & Camilla

A New Jersey Love Story2: I Got Yours, You Got Mine

A New Jersey Love Story 3: Bulletproof Love
A New Jersey Love Story 4: The Finale
Knight in Chrome: Knight & Blaize
Knight in Chrome Armor 2: Blaized Obsession
Knight in Chrome Armor 3: A Chivalrous Ending
Disturbed: An Unbalanced Love
He's Nothing Like Them Other Ones

Thank you so much for your support
With Love,

Myiesha S. Mason

Please leave your reviews on what you thought of the book
Also you can follow me on Facebook at
Myiesha Mason or join my Facebook readers group
Author Myiesha
Or Instagram at
_miss_mason
Or contact me through email at
myieshasharaemason@gmail.com

To get exclusive and advance looks

at some of our top releases:

Click the link: (App Store) http://bit.ly/2hteaH7

Click the link: (google play) http://bit.ly/2h4Jw9X

Looking for a publishing home?

Royalty Publishing House, Where the Royals reside, is accepting submissions for writers in the urban fiction genre. If you're interested, submit the first 3-4 chapters with your synopsis to submissions@royaltypublishinghouse.com. Check out our website for more information: www.royaltypublishinghouse.com.

Do You Like CELEBRITY GOSSIP? Check Out QUEEN DYNASTY!

Like Our Page HERE! Visit Our Site:

www.thequeendynasty.com

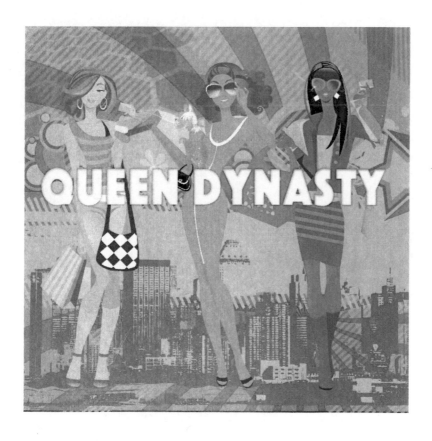

CPSIA information can be obtained
at www.ICGtesting.com
Printed in the USA
LVOW10s1727090817
544393LV00016B/1079/P